CONROY

By
Anna-Louise Dann
2019

ANNA-LOUISE DANN

To Lainey

Happy Reading

Love
Anna-Louise
x x x

Copyright © Anna-Louise Dann 2019

CONROY is dedicated to anyone out there
suffering with their mental health. Our own
minds can be our own worst enemy at times
and it's easy to allow ourselves to become
immersed in feelings of guilt, anxiety and
helplessness, we are such fragile creatures.
Sometimes we just need an understanding
ear to listen, a hand to guide us back from the
darkness and into the light. For anyone who
needs to hear this: I hope you know that you
are important, you are enough, you are loved
and when you're ready there are people who
will listen. You are not a failure, you are not
a burden and you are certainly not alone.
From one survivor to another, WE GOT THIS!

Much Love

Anna-Louise
xxx

ACKNOWLEDGEMENTS

There are so many people who I am grateful for.
I want to send out a massive thank you to everyone who picks up my books and gives them a go
even if they aren't your usual genre.
To everyone who left a review good or bad, your
feedback is invaluable to my growth as an author,
I appreciate you taking the time to let me know
what you thought.
I am inspired daily by so many different people,
their support and encouragement is what makes
me want to succeed and keep on travelling on this
crazy writing journey.
And last but by no-means least, a huge thanks
to two special ladies Lisa and Jacki for being my
"fresh eyes" you don't know how much it means
to have you take time out of your chaotic lives to
help a girl out, I am very grateful to you both.

PROLOGUE

Isla

My head hurts. I rub at my temples to try to relieve the ache. My Mother is trying and failing miserably to offer me comfort, she rubs her palm up and down my back, it's more irritating than soothing, I shift to try to escape the feeling of being touched.

The words I have been dreading for months spill from officer Beck's mouth as he fidgets with the paperwork in his hands, a sympathetic expression on his face as he feeds me the unwelcome information, the reality of his words cut me deeper than any knife ever could.

"I am so sorry it is not the news you had hoped for Miss Sussex, we have done everything we can." He looks regretful. "I am afraid with the lack of evidence we recovered it is looking more likely that Mr Peterson just doesn't want to be found."

Two days later...

The bed dips, I know who it is before she even speaks.

"Go away, Mum, I told you to just leave me be."

She sighs sadly and I feel the weight lift from the mattress. She won't listen and I don't want to be mean, I know she's worried about me, and she has every right to be-god knows I am worried about myself. I am sinking into a deep hole and there doesn't seem to be any way out.

I can't deal with other people right now, especially my Mother who is constantly fussing around me, they're all expecting me to snap out of this ruckus, smile and skip around like Daisy Fucking Sunshine.

News flash, not going to happen.

I just want Kevin to call and tell me he's alright, or walk through the door with some god-awful excuse to why he hasn't been home for four months, two weeks, three days and...I raise my head and look at my clock realising I hauled it across the room weeks ago after the cops had rung to tell me there was still no news.

I swipe away renegade tears that soak my already red and blotchy cheeks. I'm a mess, a pitiful mess of a humanbeing and I can't bring myself to care about anything but my own grief. I'm a selfish horrible person.

"Sweetheart, you need to eat, you've barely

touched any food for two days now, you're going to get sick." My Mother's fingers brush my unruly blond hair off my face, strands stick to the dried moisture stinging my skin. I look at her blankly, wishing more than anything I could take that pain from her eyes when she looks at me; but I am lost in my own world of self-loathing. Nothing is going to fill this hollow in the pit of my stomach.

Only Kevin.

One week later....

I managed to shower and brush my teeth this morning, well it was more like early afternoon; that was a feat. *Yippie for me.* I was beginning to stink. Next week I might actually manage to step a foot outside my front door. *Yeah right.* That would mean actually getting dressed and then there's that business of seeing other people. No, I am quite happy in my hovel, binge watching boxsets on Netflix and drooling over Charlie Hunnam's six pack. *Yum.*

My sister Clare walks in with my favourite mug and places the steaming hot coffee on my bedside table, I manage half a smile at her, she has been holding the fort for the last few days while Mum has been in work. I hear them talking of a night when they think I'm asleep.

They think I'll do myself some damage if I am left to my own devices-they are probably right, it wouldn't be the first time. The idea of carving up my skin to relieve some of this tension building inside me has been overwhelming just lately.

I made a promise I would never do that again. I haven't hurt myself physically since we lost dad in that awful car accident, I lost who I was for a long time afterwards, things had been on a spiral downfall before that and losing my dad had tipped me over the edge. Not now though, I am stronger than I was back then-I have to fight with every ounce of strength I can. I can't lose the last of my sanity; I am holding on so tight-if I let go, this time there won't be any coming back.

It was a dark and dangerous fall into the abyss, and I managed to drag my battered and broken psyche out of that hole and claw my way into the light. Depression with a side helping of anxiety was the devil and stole every piece of your happiness, the only thing that seemed appealing back then was checking myself out of this world.

That was six years ago now and I don't plan on traveling down that road again no matter how bad things get-and they are pretty shit.

One week and three days later...

I'm up, dressed and ready for a day on the sofa, it's been a productive hour since I rolled my lazy ass out of bed, I sigh loudly and click on the remote, channel surfing seems to be the highlight of my morning so far.

Clare is pottering about in the kitchen. It's the first day I've felt like eating anything without the thought making me want to gag.

Being the amazing big sister she is, Clare is cooking me pancakes, offering me all kinds of fruit, cream and chocolate, but as usual when I am in the mood for my favourite breakfast food I settle for crispy bacon and maple syrup, my mouth salivates and my stomach growls loudly.

I know what her game is, I am aware of how much weight I've lost, the cord on my sweats is tied as tight I can get it, I have the mini rope burns on my fingers to prove it, but they still fall down when I walk.

I tug on the loose waist band to prove a point to no one in particular. Yes, Isla you need to get out of this funk, get back to work and stop moping about.

Fuck my life.

"Isla, there's an envelope here for you, it was just posted through the door." Clare shouts from the hall pulling me out of my self-loathing, her slim frame filling the lounge doorway, her forest green eyes are full of confusion as she places the large brown and slightly crinkled envelope next to me on the love seat and then heads back to the kitchen.

I pick it up straight away eagerly tearing at the tough paper, the edge of it slices through the bend in my right index finger giving me a paper cut, I automatically pop my injured finger into my mouth, tasting the metallic taste of blood, after a couple of seconds I grow impatient and begin tearing open the envelope again, not bothered about the little smears of red I am leaving on the paper.

My hands shake as I pull out another smaller envelope inside. My name is roughly scrolled across the front and looks like it contains a letter, there is a photograph that has been enlarged onto another sheet of paper, I pull it out and I swear my heart stops for a second, my throat grows dry and my hands begin to tremble, this can't be happening.

Clear as day there is an image of Kevin sitting in the passenger seat of a black Mercedes, he is laughing at something the driver is saying, he's unharmed, healthy and has the biggest grin on his face. I process the features of the driver, he's a dark-haired male with a gruff looking beard and expensive looking sunglasses, he is smirking in Kevin's direction, they are both looking pretty pleased with themselves over something. The man isn't anyone I've met before, maybe it is one of his work colleagues?

I inspect the date.

"Mother Fucker!" I curse unable to suppress the rage building deep inside my gut I throw the paper onto the coffee table resisting the urge to tear it to pieces.

It was taken two weeks ago.

What did this mean? Who was he with? How could he do this to me?

I needed answers.

Tearing the other envelope, I pull out the slip paper with an address of a club called Rocco's, it's in Lincoln Heights on North Main Street. Written in big letters, it reads.

ASK FOR CONROY

What did that even mean?

I was damn certain I was going to find out.

CHAPTER ONE

Jamie

"You broke the law Leo, what else did you expect? If you had let me do my job like I told you to instead of losing your temper and beating the guy unconscious, you would have been on a beach somewhere with half of your divorce settlement, balls deep in Caribbean pussy. Instead, your banged up in here with a DUI and an assault charge. You're looking at some hefty fines and some serious jail time."

I stare at the pitiful douche bag behind the screen opposite me, he's holding onto the receiver like it's his lifeline, his eyes begging me for answers. I am out of solutions and patience for guys like this. Recklessly desperate and clinging to a life they used to have like it's the only thing that matters in their sorry existence.

I feel for the poor bastard, I really do, but after the mess he made of his wife's lover, this was the only place he was headed.

The guy he had beaten had looked like he had been smashed in the face with a sledge hammer a couple of times and was currently in a coma with a brain injury.

Why the hell did I bother with infidelity cases?

Seventy percent of them end like this, ok not as severe as this but someone always got either hurt or arrested. I was just landed with a shit load of paperwork to fill out and nothing to show for it, other than a headache the morning after because I usually drowned my frustrations in a bottle of Jack; in fact, the idea of Jack Daniels on the rocks was becoming more and more appealing the longer I sat in this penitentiary visiting room listening to the drone of Leo tell me how sorry he was.

I am just relieved as a business we are financially sound-we always require payment before taking cases on; otherwise this would be a whole new ball ache.

"You should have thought about the consequences of your actions Leo. I told you what would happen."

I run a frustrated hand through my hair as I watch Leo being led back to his cell. This life was becoming monotonous, the tedious cases that seemed to blend into each other were starting to ground me down; life in general was pretty unexciting, even my sex life was a chore.

I was considering finding a new hook up, Lindsey was great but I was bored with the same routine we had, we both got drunk, I fucked her and then I kicked her ass out of my apartment, I don't think we had ever banged sober. I am a self-proclaimed bachelor and I intend to use that title to its full potential.

I need something challenging, something to give me the excitement back in the pit of my stomach; I miss the buzz I used to get when I first started shadowing my dad as an impressionable teenager, before I joined the Marines.

As for women, I could pick up any woman I wanted, *shit*, I could have a new one every night, I wasn't short of propositions, but they would all end up a big disappointment. I never got serious with anyone, in fact, I can't remember the last time a woman slept in my bed for the entire night.

I wasn't the hearts and flowers type, the thought of having kids terrified me more than the fear of death. Settling down definitely wasn't an option for me.

I was an arrogant fucker, I never hid the fact, like me or not I really didn't give a fuck.

I send Greg a quick text as I head to my car, letting him know I would be back in the office soon, I had to go through a few cases before closing up shop for the day.

After the last week's clusterfuck I was seriously considering ceasing all of our infidelity cases or at least assigning another PI to them.

I climb into my Jaguar XJS and start the engine. I would never get tired of hearing the sound of her purr to life, I pat the dash board lovingly, this car had been with me though some tough times, she was my most prize possession and other than the company she was the only thing I had left of my Dad.

"Let's Go beautiful" I purr back as I reverse out of the parking space and into the LA traffic.

ΔΔΔ

I pull into my reserved space in the secured car park outside my company half an hour later. I hate this building.

My family name Conroy is on display for everyone to see; it has always been a sore point for me.

The massive letters are carved into the six-story building, making them part of the structure.

My dad had been anything but subtle when he had this place built; no expense was spared on the architects who designed this monstrous eye-sore.

I always assumed as a private investigator you had to be inconspicuous; not my old man. He wanted everyone to know when he was working a case, he believed in status, that this building put the great Mike Conroy on the map as the "Best God-damn PI this world has ever known."

My dad had been a ruthless bastard who enjoyed the fight; it was the fight that got him killed in the end. Four years, four long years, and I still hadn't given up on finding out who shot him in cold blood and dumped him in that river, every lead I have so far has came up as a dead-end.

Unlike the late-great Mike Conroy, I prefer to keep a lower profile when I am on a case, I have even taken on an alias if the investigation called for it.

The training from my time as an operative in the US army Marine Corps helps, especially when finding contacts; ten years of my life and countless missions.

I know how to blend in and take out the opposition with no fuss made. I make sure all bases are covered and I have all intel on all cases before I make my move; I can't remember the last time I took a break away from being Jamie Conroy P.I and that was just the way I liked it.

I walk through the revolving doors, passing my jacket and briefcase to Julie my PA who is ready and waiting for me with a welcoming smile, a black Americano and a list of my appointments for this afternoon. She has to almost jog to keep up with me as I power walk through the vast reception area, sipping at my coffee, while Julie runs through the schedule for the day ahead.

Different staff members greet me, I nod courteously in their direction. I have no idea who they are, or what they do here, Greg and his team are in charge of the administration and finance team, while I work with the investigation team on new cases.

I press the call button on the lift and wait impatiently, eager to get to work on the mountain of reports I have to look through.

△△△

The familiar rat-a-tat-tat on the door comes as scheduled at six. Greg breezes in not even waiting for me to invite him. What if I had been fucking a woman against this desk? I wasn't a stranger to a bit of office fun occasionally. He would have had quite the show. Knowing Greg though, he would probably enjoy being a spectator or would have asked if he could join in, this guy was all kinds of kink and one of my most trusted allies on this entire planet. I salute him as he approaches.

Greg Robert Critchley has been my best friend since my playboy college years, this guy has saved my ass more times than I can recall and vice versa. My dad gave him a job after he graduated while I was away training at the base in Afghanistan.

Greg saunters over with a bottle of scotch and two glasses, wearing the biggest shit-eating grin I had seen for a while.

"Bet you'll never guess what we're celebrating?" he asks smugly

"You finally losing your virginity?" I joke

keeping pan faced as I carry on typing up my findings from the Benson and Holland case, and their missing five hundred thousand dollars.

I have a bit more digging to do but after scouring these figures, it's looking more and more likely Holland has been transferring money into an offshore account and claiming it has been stolen. I should have the details from that account later today.

"Ha, Conroy you dick... Yeah I am now a fully-fledged whore." Greg states puffing out his chest.

"You've been a fully-fledged whore since college...what are we celebrating? I can see you're going to get your panties in a twist if you don't tell me soon."

I click save and close my laptop giving him my full attention. Greg's blue eyes lighten with excitement as he pours and hands over the generous serving of scotch; I take a huge gulp, loving the way the amber liquid burns on the journey down into my empty stomach.

"I just closed the Davies case. That tip off you gave me on Edwards sister being more involved than we thought paid off. It was her boyfriend stealing from them and she was covering for him," he explains thoughtfully.

"There was just something that didn't seem right about her when we had that meeting with her and Ed, she seemed too invested and far too emotional," I admit.

Reading people was part of my job and my gut feeling normally uncovered more than we bargained for. "So, what happens now?" I enquire taking another big gulp of scotch draining the glass.

"The boyfriend has been arrested, and the sister has been called in for questioning."

I stand patting his shoulder offering my hand for him to shake which he does vigorously.

"Congratulations my friend, I wish my day had been so successful, I need something new to focus on. I am getting bored and you know how well I respond to boredom," I grumble.

"Ah, shit man, I have the perfect cure for boredom, Senoritas and whiskey," Greg states enthusiastically shaking his hips, whiskey bottle in one hand and his freshly filled glass in the other, I chuckle and shake my head at the idiot.

"Just give me another hour to finish this report and we'll head over to Rocco's for a few."

I have to get this finished, I won't be able to sleep tonight if I have a half-written report waiting for me.

Greg salutes me with a cheesy grin before dancing his way out of the door.

CHAPTER TWO

Jamie

The smell of tobacco and stale spirits coats the evening air as I exit the cab outside The Rocco Club on Main Street.

Antonio Rocco only allows prepaid guests A-listers or family into his award-winning establishment.

Fortunately for me I was the latter.

Antonio is my mamma's brother and was best friends with my dad, they all grew up together.

The old man was a businessman first, ruthless and moody as fuck, but he would lay down his life for his family and friends.

This club had become his entire life after my Aunt Viola died. Watching the woman, he loved suffer like she did took the light from his eyes. Witnessing the cancer quickly infesting her weak, fragile body, while all he could do was sit there hopelessly holding her hand, wishing things were different.

Seeing one of the strongest men I knew go

through something like that was a hard thing to deal with, even for a heartless bastard like me.

Cancer was ruthless, it took no prisoners and didn't care who it hurt, my Aunt was a wonderful woman and didn't deserve to go like that.

I had watched my uncle who was far from being a religious man, praying daily in the hospital chapel for some divine being to just take all the pain away. She died, and he was a shell of a man for a long time after, the arrogant stubborn asshole we have all come to love emerged later, he was now a far cry from the lovable *furfante* we used to know.

Watching my Uncles world turn so devastatingly has cemented my notions of marriage, that and the shambles my parents marriage turned out to be. My Dad was married to the job and my Momma enjoyed the company of younger men, she was currently on husband number four, a fashion designer from Madrid.

No, I wouldn't be stupid enough to get involved that deep with a woman; falling in love made you vulnerable.

scanning the outside of the building I follow the pattern of the original brick work which has been restored to its former glory. I couldn't believe it was still intact after all this time, this really was an impressive place.

The red carpet leading to the entrance was used only by the more elite guests. I was just as fucking elite as the assholes that would be inside, waving their golden balls at any female who caught their eye. Unfortunately for the Fat Cats with their tiny peckers it was normally me escorting those females out of the door, with Mr Bling left out in the cold wondering why his multi-million-dollar cock didn't buy him some classy pussy for the night. The Conroy charm was all I needed to score a lay for the night, plus, I could read those women like a book.

I knew women; I liked women, and if they wanted me with no strings attached, why not enjoy the spoils of being a bachelor?

My training had taught me to read people to infiltrate the enemy, except these days the only thing I was infiltrating were thieves and cheating spouses.

The skills I had learnt were something that never went away, at times they were more of an inconvenience. I could read people and situations. A slight flick of the hand or the twitch of someone's eye could tell me everything I needed to know about someone.

The pulse at the side of their neck, sweat beads forming on their brow or the grip of the hand on a glass as they spoke. There were so many simple ways to figure out how genuine a person was or what their intentions were.

Greg referred to me many times as a human lie detector; it had been both a blessing and a curse over the years.

This is why my circle was small and this

was why I didn't keep relationships, I could read their intentions as soon as I engaged in conversation with a female, the dilation of her pupils, the change in breathing, even the tilt of her hips indicated whether she was up for a night of sexual exploration with me, or whether she was on the prowl for something more permanent, unlucky for them they never lasted more than one night in my bed, I was a cold-hearted bastard and I wasn't about to change for anyone, I liked my life exactly the way it was; besides, I didn't have time to entertain or commit to a woman.

I take in the building in front of me for a second. The old rundown movie theatre has an old-world vibe. The spectacular building was built in the nineteen-twenties and was originally one of the first movie theatres built in the Lincoln Heights area, it had been derelict when my Uncle bought it in the early eighties. The rustic decor on the outside has been restored to its full glory. The billboards which hang flush against the old brickwork had the ever-changing images of the singers and bands my Uncle has performing here. The big lettering that once read *Beaumont Theatre* were replaced with Rocco's.

I look at my watch; I had waited here long enough for Greg; the bystanders waiting to get past the strict security are looking at me weirdly and I am bored shitless.

"Conroy." Greg's voice has me whipping my head around.

"What took you so long? I was starting to feel like a jilted prom date," I joke, earning a grin. I would die for this guy but his time keeping was shit.

"You would make one butt ugly woman." Here comes the banter that always got us through every day.

"Probably, but you still would. I've got a pulse, haven't I?" I mock, smirking.
Greg places his hand to his heart batting his lashes while giving me his best innocent face and I snort.

"Conroy, I don't know what you mean, I am still a virgin," he scoffs giving me the doe-eyes.

We both lose it laughing.

This is what it was like with us, we never argued, never fell out. We had experienced and seen so much shit together we knew what each-other was thinking at times.

I slap his back affectionately.

"Let's get in before Antonio sends his security out to chase us off for loitering," I muse, heading down the carpet to the entrance.

"Yeah, let's not piss Uncle Rocco off. He's a mean old bastard."

He wasn't wrong.

The club was a little quieter tonight. I sit in my usual place at the bar people watching while Greg is keeping himself amused chatting up an attractive brunette on the other end of the bar. She is wearing a red dress that looks about two sizes too small for her, Greg liked them blatant, I preferred them with more class and a little harder to get.

Taking a sip of my Jack Daniels on the rocks, I scan the club spotting a group of women dancing provocatively, rolling their hips to the song being played by the house band. There are two young men watching them, waiting for their chance to swoop in and hook up with one of them. I swear it was tragic how desperate some of these guys were.

A movement catches my eye from the other end of the room.

The most beautiful woman I have seen in a long time stands looking lost and I find myself wondering if she's with anyone. Her light blond hair is loosely curled over her petite shoulders, the black tight dress she is wearing hugs her slim waist flaring out at the curve of her hips showcasing her hourglass figure, the heart shape bodice allows a subtle hint of enough cleavage to make me want to see more, she would be so much fun to unwrap.

But it is her face that draws me in the most, she's got the cutest little dimple in her chin, full red lips, high cheekbones, her nose is small and straight, and those eyes, I couldn't make out the color, they were wide, cautious and now looking straight at me, as one of my Uncles security nervously gestures in my direction.

I watch her walk, the natural sway of her hips, a half tilt of her lips and the tight grip she has on her black clutch bag is an indication of her nervousness. As she approaches, I stand to greet her ever being the gentleman.

"Mr Conroy?" She asks unsure, her voice is deep and quivers slightly; her small hand shoots out to shake mine, something flashes across her features, she is embarrassed by her reaction. My huge palm engulfs her tiny fingers, I feel a slight tremor in her hand.

Her eyes are the deepest forest green and unbelievably breath-taking, for the first time in my life I feel a little nervous myself and I have to swallow before I speak.

"That's me. What can I do for you Miss?" I ask keeping hold of her small hand, it feels good in mine, too good.

I wonder what those hands would feel like wrapped around my cock.

My cock certainly liked that idea.

I have a feeling that wasn't in her plans for this evening though, she had obviously come here to ask me to help her with something, her eyes are full of fear, I see something very familiar in their depths.

"My name's Isla, Isla Sussex and I believe you can help me find my missing fiancé."

The night just got a lot more interesting.

CHAPTER THREE

Isla

My stomach is in knots. Just being here alone is enough to drive my anxiety to a colossal level, especially after all the fun Clare had getting me tickets into this place. It was more secure than Alcatraz, with the amount of security you had to go through just to get through the door.

I had been frisked thoroughly by the oversized man beast who looked like his skin was about to tear through the black suit he was wearing. I had to bite my lip from asking why Mr Muscle hadn't bought me a drink first, as he had patted me down over enthusiastically with his mammoth sized paws.

Entering the bar area, I look around at the old curved woodwork that I was certain was part of the original fixtures of the place, the intricate decorative detail presented a class from a time long ago.

Apparently, this was the "Place to be." I didn't see the appeal myself, I mean it was a beautiful building, the history alone was inter-

esting, and me being a bit of an American history nerd I am not ashamed to say the idea of
coming here had peaked my weird obsession with
the restoration of an old building, I had traveled
to different continents to stare in awe at ancient
architecture, so visiting this place under different
circumstances would be a treat, especially during
the day-light so I could look around properly.

My distaste wasn't the magnificent inter-
ior; it was all the stuck up, Yankie aristocrats
and their inability to keep their hands to themselves. They assumed because they had dollars on
tap; they were invincible and could own anything
they desired. I'd already been propositioned as I
walked in here, like I was some back-room whore.
Three times by three different men all vile a-holes
with bad breath and a predatory glint in their
eye–I had only been in here twenty minutes. No,
I wouldn't be coming back here ever again not by
choice anyway, no matter how intrigued I was by
the vintage decor.

Clare's boyfriend James was good friends
with one of the managers here and had arranged
two tickets for us, they hadn't been cheap, it was
extortionate for a night out here. I was lucky I had
some money saved from the modelling work I did
before Kevin disappeared, I also had the money
from when our dad died, he had left me and Clare
with enough cash to set us up for our future. Although, I could think of better things I would rather be spending my inheritance on; like a holiday

or a new car. But, as usual my inability to let things go had put me in a position, a position I was now beginning to regret.

Lord help me, I had to have answers before I could move on, I had to find out why Kevin had disappeared without so much as a goodbye.

I needed to find this Conroy, I scanned the room, not quite sure where to begin, A guy wearing a suit with a security badge walks past me, I had to get this over with so I could get out of here.

"Excuse me sir?" I call, he whips around scowling, the annoyance of being interrupted turns into a predatory smile when his eyes land on me. *Creep.*

"What can I do for you pretty lady, is someone giving you trouble?" He waves his eyebrows seductively at me. As much as I wanted too, I couldn't tell him to go fuck himself, so I plaster on a sickly-sweet smile.

"I am looking for someone called Conroy, I was told I would find them here?"

His entire body language changes; his eyes lose the playfulness, replaced by something else, respect or fear maybe?

"You're in luck Miss, Conroy is sitting at the bar over there." He points to a dark haired man sitting at the bar before walking off abruptly, he doesn't give me a chance to thank him.

My attention is now directed to the bar where my eyes meet with the most gorgeous looking man, his gaze sends a flutter into the pit of my stomach. My feet gravitate towards him shamelessly. I remind myself why I came here and it definitely wasn't to ogle handsome strangers, even if they were as mouth-watering as the man in front of me.

I need an explanation and according to that letter, this gorgeous six foot of Italian, dark-haired hotness could help me get my answers. Now I was here he really wasn't what I had been expecting...

I reach Mr tall dark and handsome pushing my left hand out towards him awkwardly.

"Mr Conroy?"

This definitely isn't one of my finest moments. I am sure my cheeks are crimson.

As soon as his palm touches mine the fluttering in my stomach catapults into overdrive, his dark eyes bore into mine like he's figured me out already, I am certain he can probably feel my hand shake in his.

I really need to calm down and take control of my nerves. I need this man to help me.

"What can I do for you, Miss?" He asks, a welcoming smile on his perfect lips. His voice is sexy, deep, rich and well-spoken with an ever so slight hint of an Italian intonation.

"My name's Isla, Isla Sussex and I believe you can help me find my missing fiancé." I was unable to hide the Louisiana drawl as I spoke; it always crept out when I was nervous, despite the several years of vocal training my father had insisted on.

I subconsciously high-five myself for completing a sentence though. This guy is seriously distracting me.

The first thing that draws my attention is his beautiful olive skin, I am not sure why but it evokes memories of the little holidays we used to take in Naples when I was a teenager, there were a few times me and Clare would be entranced by the handsome boys splashing about topless in the sea as we basked in the Mediterranean sunshine.

My eyes roam his gorgeous chiselled features, his full lips, high cheekbones, and hypnotic brown eyes which seem to look straight through me. The way he's watching almost has me convinced he can read my wayward thoughts...and as if on cue he grins lighting up all the darkness in his eyes. *Perfection*.

I am sure my heart is about to implode from all the beating it is currently doing in my chest, I swear it is going to hammer its way out of there any second, I resist the urge to press my hand there to check or fan myself.

He lets go of my hand, and I mercilessly grip my clutch, finding comfort in squeezing the leather, the rubbery material reminds me of the stress ball I have been using at home, which brings me a little comfort.

"You look nervous, Miss Sussex," he acknowledges, amusement in his tone...hmm the man was observant.

"I am," I admit. "I've never done this before, and I wasn't sure how to approach you. You see, I got your details from an anonymous source and I was told to come here and ask for you. It is unusually spontaneous for me. I–Er don't normally do things at the spur of the moment like this, but I need answers. My sister was supposed to be with me, but she had something come up."

I know am rambling like I always do when I am nervous, but I've learnt to just go with it and hope I don't embarrass myself completely.

His expression is unwavering, like he doesn't notice or doesn't care about my inability to hit the pause button. His brows suddenly furrow, and I am damned if it doesn't make him look even more sexy.

Jeez, even frowning this guy is hot.

"I see... Well Miss Sussex the usual protocol for hiring a private investigator is, you usually arrange a meeting at a time and place which is convenient for both parties," he declares.

He's a private investigator? *Shit,* I knew this was a bad idea. I should apologize and leave, like now. I'll get out of here before I make an even bigger fool of myself. I am certain my cheeks are glowing with embarrassment.

"Of course," I squeak and clear my throat. "It was very rude of me to ambush you while you are obviously busy. I am sorry to have taken up your time, Mr Conroy." I offer an apologetic smile. I really want the ground to swallow me up about now.

I turn on my heel to walk away.

"Miss Sussex, are you leaving so soon? I was quite enjoying being ambushed by you," he calls after me, stopping me in my tracks.

I turn around to throw some clever flirty line back but collide with his chest as he steps forward. I put my hand out to save myself and find hard muscled abs underneath my palm with only a thin barrier of material between our skin. I curse my clumsiness and lift my head to apologize. I am so flustered and panting; another side effect of my nerves.

I am met with Mr Conroy's sexy smirk, laughter dances in his gaze, his right hand is on my left hip steadying me in our collision.

He doesn't release me immediately.

The warmth from his hand penetrates through my dress and heats my skin sending waves of pleasure to my core, igniting something in me. A woodsy and bergamot scent drift up my welcoming nostrils. His smell and touch are intoxicating, addictive and dangerous for a girl like me.

"My name is Jamie Conroy of Conroy Investigations and it would be my pleasure to help you Miss Sussex. Now, would you like to have a drink with me?"

CHAPTER FOUR

Jamie

Powering up my laptop on my coffee table. I pace back and forth, I need to decide what research to start first, taking a sip of my freshly filled glass of whiskey, I stare out of my balcony window at the clear Los Angeles skyline.

My head is full of unanswered questions. As exhausted as I am, I can't settle.

I haven't felt this pumped about a case for a long time.

Something is bugging me though, this isn't going to be a typical missing person case. Whoever sent those pictures to Isla had mentioned my name. Someone wanted me to take this case, and I have every intention of finding out who that is, it's left me feeling uneasy and just a little excited about digging deeper into this whole thing.

I pull up Isla's social media accounts, I'm impressed at how secure they are; all of her privacy setting are in place. The only way anyone can gain access is through friend requests. The only thing visible to anyone looking for her is her name and profile picture; the image is of her and a woman with similar features, they are both smiling widely as they pose for the selfie. This must be her sister Clare. Was this always her profile picture or had she changed it once she realise her fiance was playing her?

Sitting with little Miss Sussex at the bar for the best part of two hours had been very informative, she was forthcoming in her family life and her career choices. Her face and soft voice were ingrained into my brain. I had studied the delicate way she ran her fingers along her lips when she was thinking of what to say next, the way her nose crinkled when she laughed, or the way her perfect porcelain skin grew pink when she rambled for longer than she intended.

She hid behind her sweet smile and her awkwardness but I had seen the torture in the depths of her eyes, the way her fingers held her clutch in a death like grip to suppress the need to escape, the slight shake of her fingers as she lifted her wine glass to her gorgeous full lips.

The faint scarring on her wrists and forearms told their own tale of a dark history. She had been through something, some time ago judging by the scar tissue on her right forearm, the faded white lines were evidence of a few years of self-harm. I admire her for not attempting to cover them up; although, the thought of her hurting herself pulled at something deep inside me, I take another gulp of my whiskey and tap my forefinger against the glass.

The demons were still there behind her eyes, gnawing away at her; I could sense she had been struggling with them lately, especially when she talked about her fiance Kevin. The dark circles around her eyes and the chewed thumb nail on her right hand which she had tried to cover up with red nail polish were a big indication of anxiety. I bet that asshole disappearing had thrown in a heap of self-doubt as well.

I knew better than anyone what it was like when you allowed that darkness to creep in; it happened slowly until it took you over creating a dysfunctional, destructive existence were the only thing that suppressed the demons for a little while was pain, carving up your skin to release the pressure inside. I never took a blade to my skin, I just spent most days in the beginning with a gun pressed to my temple, daring myself to pull that trigger and end the chaos inside my head.

I would bet this Kevin disappearing was poking at the side of herself she had worked so hard to bury.

Those demons they never went away, they ingrained themselves into your very fabric becoming part of you, it took a lot of therapy and self-belief to claw out of that pit.

People saw you as weak, broken and selfish or looked at you with pity; neither was helpful. The battle against your own mind is one of the toughest forms of combat a person can face.

I fought similar demons after being forced to leave my position in the military. Throwing myself back into civilian life had been challenging, I had locked myself away, suffered from recurring nightmares of that horrendous bus explosion.

A shudder wracks my body, the screams and the smell of scorched flesh penetrate my senses as I dragged burnt children's corpses out of that vehicle, praying to anyone who could hear me that I find just one survivor; even my own life-threatening injuries couldn't have stopped me that day. The doctors told me I was lucky to be alive, lucky the shrapnel missed vital nerves in my back, I resist the urge to reach behind and run my fingers down the scar tissue, reliving the entire thing again like I did everyday of my life.

I wasn't lucky, there's nothing lucky about witnessing something like that. Those kids didn't deserve to die…

I was diagnosed with PTSD and unfit to return to service, typical fucking doctors and their labels, labels that stuck and defined how your life would become; an endless battle against a system that would eventually deem you as pathetic as you felt.

The first two years were the worst, I was weak and useless, a waste of space. If rock bottom was a thing to aim for; I had surpassed it more times than I care to recall…That was over eight years ago now, the thought of blowing my own skull open isn't as appealing as it once was. Taking over my Dad's company gave me back my sanity; well, enough to function as a reasonably 'normal' humanbeing. As much as I detest some cases at times, they are the reason I can still wake up every day. Putting my military training into use when working on cases has given me a purpose. *Once a Marine always a Marine.*

I rarely switch off from that part of myself.

Months of therapy and countless meetings made me realise I wasn't weak or useless, to come out the other end of that black hole... I was a tough fucker, there wasn't much that could beat me anymore. I drain the rest of my glass and salute to my reflection in the large window.

I allowed my wayward thoughts to drift back to Isla; I didn't like to dwell on the past for too long and Miss Sussex was a welcoming distraction.

After talking to her about our common interests of old buildings, she had only grown on me more. Listening to her talk enthusiastically about her love of architecture and her family's Southern heritage had me wanting to sit and talk with her for hours, catching the unintentional sexy Louisiana twang which escaped occasionally. I found myself wanting to know everything about the beautiful intriguing woman sitting across from me.

I walked her to a cab afterwards before heading back , I am not ashamed to admit my disappointment at watching her drive away. Athough, I would never admit that to anyone.

We have arranged to meet at my office first thing Monday morning to discuss business. She was emailing the image she had received to my company email address, so I could get the license plate checked out. Just the thought of seeing her again stirred something inside of me. This was a strange situation for me, no one got under my skin ever; certainly never after one meeting. The scent of her floral perfume still lingered in my senses, her face so close to mine. I resisted the urge to claim those beautiful, full, red lips. The thought of just kissing her was giving me an erection as hard as a rock, I bet she tasted as good as she looked. *Fuck.*

I hadn't felt the need to bring a hook-up home, even the familiar booty-call from Lindsey went unanswered when she had blown my phone up with her usual messages.

Greg had accused me of being ill before he took home his playmate for the evening. The brunette had clung to him like a second skin, lapping up every line he fed her. I really wasn't in the mood for false pretenses tonight. The last thing I needed right now was a distraction when I had so much to get straight in my own head. Maybe I was off my game? My mind is in turmoil.

Who is this dumb bastard Kevin? What part did he have to play? Why he would walk away from someone like Isla?

Fuck, there she is again, back in my head, the woman has caught me off guard; she wasn't my usual clientele, she hadn't even known I was a P.I, that had been obvious by the change in her body language when I had introduced myself properly; the way she blushed and fidgeted when I teased her. *Jeez* she was about the cutest damn thing.

She was the whole package, gorgeous, smart and genuine, she had a smile you could get lost in. There was a vulnerability surrounding her that had awakened the protector in me and that body, *fuck*. I had reminded my dick on numerous occasions that she was a client and out of bounds. Although, the sultry way her pupils dilated and the little intake of air when my body was pressed against hers told me she was just as attracted to me.

The reminder of having her moulded against me, her curves fit so perfectly, I groan out loud. Relieving the ache in my balls would have to wait until later.

I have work to do.

Women like Miss Isla Sussex didn't come

around very often, I was damned well going to find out every little thing about her and this dickhead she had gotten herself involved with.

I have a feeling she isn't going to like what I uncover, and I could sense I wasn't going to come out of this case unscathed.

CHAPTER FIVE

Isla

I stare at the escalator door willing it to open so I can jump in before anyone else joins me.

Looking around the building, it seems empty apart from a few security guards and a few receptionists.

I've arrived forty-five minutes early so I can avoid sharing the claustrophobic metal contraption with anyone. My palms are growing damp at the thought of stepping a foot in the darn thing. I would have taken the stairs, but it is twenty-one degrees outside, and I am already starting to perspire. I am wearing my new nude heels and I haven't broken them in properly yet, so that is a blister waiting to happen.

Heat, stairs, and heels were not a good combination at any time for someone as unfit as me, but certainly not for a serious meeting with the infamous Jamie Conroy. I am trying to look half decent and retain a business-like rapport, and the humidity is already taking its toll. If I rocked in with sweat stains, runny eye make-up and fizzy hair I would die of embarrassment.

I smooth the fabric of my sleeveless, white pencil dress down and adjust the plastic folder in my arms already regretting my choice of outfit for today's meeting. Knowing my luck, I would probably end up staining the white material before the morning was through.

The doors open, I step in and press the button for the fifth floor trying to calm the anxiety bubbling in my chest; taking a few deep breaths as I white knuckle the piece of thin plastic in my hands; my mantra does'nt seem to be working this morning. I seriously need to calm down before I make a complete show of myself.

Thankfully, the doors close and I am left alone. I blow out a sigh of relief some of the tension falling away.

Other than pictures of the Conroy building there had been nothing, nada, zilch of Jamie online, with a company this big though surely, he's been photographed?

I would never admit it out loud, but the man has affected me more than I am comfortable with. I spent most of yesterday scouring social media and Google for any trace of Mr Conroy. My stalker game is so weak, but the lack of information has left me more intrigued.

I had spent the rest of the day feeling guilty and hating myself for even thinking of another man while Kevin is still incognito.

I am a glutton for punishment when it comes to Kevin and the hold, he's always had on me, a hold I am not sure was entirely healthy now I've had time to reflect on everything. It's amazing how anger and betrayal can open your eyes to other things I had overlooked before.

This was the first time in four years that another man has turned my head, and why shouldn't he when he is as hot and broody as Mr Conroy. I resist the urge to fake fan myself. Jamie Conroy is a hard man to forget, he even managed to creep into my dreams last night, my cheeks heat with the reminder of his hands and lips–no, I had to stop thinking about him like that; I need his help; I love Kevin, don't I?... Of course, I do. Once Kevin is home everything will be ok again...

The escalator doors open, and I step into the cool reception area taking a minute to appreciate the air-con.

A beautiful red head sits at the desk typing away at her computer, her auburn curls bounce as she looks up and smiles warmly.

"You must be Miss Sussex. My name is Harriet. Mr Conroy did mention you might be early; he will be with you shortly. Please take a seat." She indicates to the small waiting area, "could I get you a drink Mam?" Harriet offers. I recognize that familiar drawl. Was she a Louisiana girl like me? I wasn't brave enough to begin a conversation even though she seems pleasant enough.

"Could I just have some water, please?" I answer, returning the warm smile as I walk cautiously to the comfortable looking seats.

How the hell did he know I would be here earlier?

Jamie

I am running on Espresso. Caffeine is my best friend today. This case had me crawling the walls until four this morning. The more I uncovered about this fucking douche-bag Kevin, the more uneasy I felt.

The guy was running with some bad people, people he had no business getting into bed with. They were the kind of men who would slit their own mother's throat if the price was high enough.

My contacts within the DEA had run the plates on the car and traced it to a Marcus Ravenstone a well-known drug lord, human trafficker and cop killer. Ravenstone was responsible for the brutal torture and killing of four DEA agents a few months ago in the LA area, those bodies had been unrecognisable when they pulled the scattered disembodied limbs from the several dumpsters around the city.

These weren't the type of guys you could play friends with. Either Kevin was an active part of his gang or he had stupidly got himself involved by mistake. Either way, I wouldn't take any chances, if Kevin turned out to be a threat, I am more than willing to off the motherfucker, my Glock hasn't been used for a while, and I am itching to warm it up.

The more I thought of anything happening to Isla because of that weasel the more my gut knotted, this feeling was unusual, I didn't connect with women on any level other than us both getting off, but Miss Sussex had peaked my interest.

Getting any kind of information about Kevin's whereabouts these last few months was going to be dangerous, I am going to have to go deep and involve some trust worthy friends to get the information I need.

I am off out to a biker bar downtown later to see what I can find out. Razor is meeting me there to point me in the right direction, he's a friend I haven't seen for a while, so this should be an interesting night.

I press print on all the paperwork I have so far to add it to the file I am putting together.

Just as I am about to pour myself another espresso the phone on my desk rings, I lift the receiver.

"Your nine o'clock is here Mr Conroy," Harriet drawls. I check my watch, she's forty-five minutes early like I suspected she would be.

"Thank you Harriet, I'll be out in a moment, don't send her in."

The reception area is quiet. Harriet looks up and grins at me when I enter, she's aware I don't normally leave my office to greet the clients and obviously finds this amusing, I send a warning glare in her direction and give a little shake of my head, it works and she pretends to look down at something on her desk.

Isla sits engrossed in the file she's holding, one leg crossed over the other exposing some of her lower thigh, I watch her intently for a few seconds taking in the mesmerising sight of Miss Isla Sussex; she really is a vision.

I clear my throat loudly and she raises her head from the file on her lap, emerald eyes full of uncertainty meet mine. I smile.

"Miss Sussex, it's really good to see you again, please follow me into my office."

The slight nod of her head as she stands gracefully from her sitting position and the slight tremor in her hands; she is unable to hide the nervousness in her body language, the grip she has on that file tightens, the way her shoulders are lowered, cautious eyes dart around the room, it's like she's waiting for something bad to happen or looking for an exit strategy.

I don't blame her though, I do the same when I visit new places, it's always good to know the best way out if anything goes wrong.

"I-it's er good to see you too Mr Conroy... I

brought some information that might help." Her smile waivers.

"That's great, I have set up a file of my own, I think you'll be satisfied with my progress so far... Please come this way Miss Sussex. I don't want to discuss your business out here."

Her cheeks darken slightly "Of course," she says as she walks towards me. She really is beautiful. The images I have of her don't do her justice, even her modelling portfolio pictures were nothing compared to the real thing, she is naturally captivating.

That dress clings to her like second skin, the white material giving her an angelic glow.

The next few hours are going to be torture of the best kind.

"Could you bring us in some refreshments, and please see to it I am not disturbed by anyone." I tell Harriet on my way past.

"Of course, Mr Conroy," Harriets fake sing-song voice and grin, grinds my gears and I send her another warning look, she was in a particularly annoyingly humourous mood this morning and I didn't have the time or the patience to play along today.

If I wanted to get to know this perfect creature better, I couldn't have any distractions.

God knows she is distracting enough.

CHAPTER SIX

Isla

Jamie's office is enormous and stylishly decorated, the entire room oozes wealth and power. I wasn't expecting something as impressive as this, I mean this room is bigger than my entire apartment. A massive black desk sits in the middle of the vast floor space, behind it the big windows let in the morning light. There are two black expensive looking sofa's and matching chairs on the far side of the room with a glass coffee table hosting a beautiful crystal vase resting in the center, it has the most beautiful pink lilies I have ever seen. The fresh flowers perfume the air adding a sweet floral scent. The fragrance compliments the familiar woodsy smell coating my nostrils.

The seductive masculine aroma of Jamie Conroy invades my senses making me fully aware of his closeness behind me. I am certain his scent will be ingrained into my memory for all eternity. Butterflies dance in my stomach with anticipation as I slowly walk further into the room.

He's quiet as if he's allowing me a few seconds to take in the magnitude of this room.

"This is an impressive workspace Mr Conroy." I blurt out, my Louisiana drawl creeps in, I am unable to disguise the quiver of nerves in my voice, I'm surprised I can even speak at all, with him so close to me.

"Thank you, Miss Sussex, it was originally my Fathers, I am considering sectioning it off to create more offices, this is far too big and very pretentious. My father liked to make sure everyone knew who he was, this office is evidence of that. I prefer to keep my business a little more inconspicuous and out of the public eye, after all how can you call yourself a P.I if the whole of America knows what you look like." A frown furrows on his brow after his little outburst and he clears his throat. "Please take a seat on one of the sofas over there, I will bring my file over in a moment and we can get started."

I sense distain in his tone when he spoke about his father, there was obviously some bad history between them. I think better about asking. I learnt at a young age that business and family never ran smoothly together; my dad taught me that.

I walk to one of the sofas and sit, removing the photograph and all the paperwork I have on Kevin. I place the empty file on the coffee table.

Now my hands are free I am feeling rather anxious at not having my plastic shield anymore. My inner mantra to try and calm myself isn't working today.

"Are you feeling ok Miss Sussex? You look like you are about to throw up." Jamie's deep voice pulls me from my state of panic and the fog clears slightly, his tone is soothing and surprisingly I begin to calm a little.

"I-I. Could I just have some water please?" I ask weakly. This really isn't how I pictured this meeting.

"Certainly, would you like to reschedule if you're not feeling well?" *Jeez.* It had taken enough courage to come here today.

"I'll be ok in a moment," I assure him beginning to relax a little.

Talking to him was a lot easier than I thought, he didn't look at me like I was losing my mind, which is usually the response I get when my anxiety hits. No, he is looking at me like he understands, empathy radiates from him; this gives me the confidence to confide in him, my confession starts pouring out of me before I can stop it.

"I used to suffer with anxiety a long time ago after my dad died, it got pretty severe. Kevin's disappearance has caused a relapse, I am nowhere near as bad as I used to be, I've learnt different coping methods to handle things when they get bad. Sometimes the silliest thing can trigger it though. I'm sorry I am rambling, that's another part of it, I can't get myself to stop talking, you must think I'm a nut job." *Fuck.* Well done Isla, way to redeem yourself as a stable individual.

"Is that where you got your scars from?" Jamie asks me, his question takes my focus away from my entwined fingers, his face is full of concern. Nope, still no judgement in the depths of his gorgeous brown eyes, just that understanding I'm beginning to warm to.

Had he really noticed the faint scarring on my arms? It was such a long time ago now, I didn't think about them anymore, at least not very often anyway.

"I-I used to self-harm." My voice is almost a whisper.

He covers the distance between us and within a second, he's sitting next to me my heart pounds in my chest as his fingers reach out to trace the faded silver lines on my right arm, I tense waiting for the feeling of his fingers on my skin. His hand pulls back last minute, his expression perturbed.

"I have PTSD," he says catching me off guard with his honesty. "It's manageable now, but like yourself at one stage it got pretty fucked up," he confesses. There's a haunted look on his handsome face, he's recalling bad memories. It's my turn to empathise with him and show him some of that understanding back.

Life can be so cruel sometimes, and it seems like we've both been dealt a raw deal. I would love to find out more about him, but I don't want to push the subject. Judging by the look on his face, he was already regretting spilling so much about himself.

A person's mental health is such a fragile thing at times, and he had obviously been through a lot in his life.

My heart breaks for him. I want to try and comfort him in some way, but I am lost for words. This was intense for our first meeting and we hadn't even discussed the case yet.

His eyes meet mine, he's so close, goose bumps prickle my skin as he opens his mouth to say something.

"We all have demons Miss Sussex some will consume us but only if we allow them too."

He stands creating distance between us; it is probably a good idea, the sensations cursing through my body at just having him sit next to me are disconcerting and knowing that he understands the reason behind the madness inside my head only makes me more attracted to him.

He clears his throat again, "Now let me get you that water and I'll show you what I've found on Kevin so far."

I nod unable to form a coherent sentence.

Jamie

"As you can see Miss Sussex, Kevin has been inhabiting with some people you don't want to mess with. In fact, before four years ago there's no record of your Kevin Peterson anywhere, which seems very strange."

Her cheeks are flushed, she looks worried; but I was expecting a bigger reaction to 'your fiancé is running around with the Cartel'.

"That is strange, do you think he is one of them?" She inquires as chews on her bottom lip; I resist the urge to place my finger where her teeth gnaw away. The thought of having her full mouth against any part of my anatomy has my dick waking up as if it's volunteering. I shift uncomfortably to hide my growing need. I'm not a fucking saint and I've had no action this weekend, which is a first for me, so having a woman as beautiful as Isla sitting opposite me batting those big green eyes is doing things to my libido.

I really need to get laid.

"I am not a hundred percent yet. I have a few theories about it, but I can't say for certain. I have a contact I am meeting with later tonight at The JoJo club, I should have more information then."

Her brows raise, something flashes in her eyes. "Do you think I am in any danger from these men he's working with?" She questions.

"I doubt they are even aware of your existence." I reassure her. Although, they probably know everything about her and her entire family, especially if Kevin is in as deep as I suspect, they'll need leverage if he goes rogue.

My reassurance seems to appease her for now, but I have a feeling Miss Sussex already knows there's more to this than I am willing to divulge. I've already spilled enough today. What is it about this woman that makes me want to share the darkest parts of myself with her? Only a few people know about my PTSD, Isla was now one of them; something about her had me spilling all of my secrets.

There's a unspoken connection, an understanding between us. I have to watch what I share from now on. She caught me off guard today. I blame lack of sleep. My loose tongue could lead to my demise with this woman.

Isla Sussex was my client and I had to remain professional, no matter how much I wanted to see what was underneath those classy little dresses she wears.

CHAPTER SEVEN

Jamie

I pull into the car park outside JoJo's, get out and close the door gently, making sure my beauty is locked. Pushing my wallet and keys into the pocket of my leather jacket. I walk the short distance to the club, my senses are on high alert. I often wonder what it would feel like to be able to just switch off and not always be looking over my shoulder; that would never be my life.

JoJo's is known for being a meeting place for the less than upstanding members of the LA community, but it wasn't so bad when you knew people here, the owner was an old friend of my dad's. Anyone who tried anything would be a sorry sonofabitch, but that didn't stop assholes from trying.

The line of custom-made Harley Davidson's covering the sidewalk are a welcoming sight. The emblem of the howling wolf on the tank puts me at ease, tonight should run smoothly. Razor should be with them. Richie Marland aka Razor is the Vice President for The Maw of Fenris Mc and an old Marine brother of mine. If I needed information about the Cartel and their members, this was the club to go to. The Fenris and a few other Mc's were currently "Doing deals" with the Cartel and Razor was their source for gathering important intel.

Even with a prosthetic leg Razor was the toughest son of a bitch I knew. The same explosion which had taken my sanity had robbed him of his leg. We had both been in a bad way after our service ended so abruptly, but we had sworn no matter what happened after, we would always have each other's back, there was only two men I trusted with my life and Razor was one of them.

Nodding a greeting to the familiar security on the door I enter the club, eager to get this over with.

The scent of stale booze and sweat coats the musky, dim lit bar area. There are a few couples swaying to an old slow country song playing on the battered jukebox in the corner.

I order myself a beer and scan the room for Razor and his boys. There's no sign. They must be in the pool area. The guys liked challenging customers on the pool tables, which normally meant they walked away with a nice roll of dollars at the end of the night. I have no doubt that's where they'll all be. I pay for my beer and make my way through the double doors into the huge games room.

There is a table in the far end with a group

playing poker, I notice one of The Fenris prospects sitting with them, one of the club whores is draped seductively over the back of his chair.

There are eight pool tables filling up the rest of the room, each one is filled with regulars and bikers. I spot Razor straight away he is standing at the back of the room leaning against the wall, smirking down at a fiery blond giving him hell, she is poking at his chest cussing him out for something he'd said.

I walk over grinning, trust Razor to rub a woman up the wrong way, he never was subtle with his affection for the opposite sex. By the way the little firecracker is going to town on him it looks like he's found one immune to him. Razor looks up at me an amused glint in his eye. "Does this little Southern Wild Cat belong to you JC? She's all teeth and spitfire."

The woman turns looking pissed and I can't breathe for a second, my jaw drops as big familiar green eyes bore into mine.

The tight blue jeans fit her far too well, hugging her pert little butt in all the right places, the black torn t-shirt she is wearing has Born Wild stamped across her ample tits in faded grey writing, the slash marks through it give me a welcoming flash of her assets. Her flat stomach is bare, the show of her gorgeous flesh makes me want to forget she's my client and give in to the hunger that's been building inside since meeting this beautiful creature.

She is completely different from the classy woman in white sitting in my office this morning the vulnerable and angelic beauty has been replaced by this wild and sassy tigress.

I am impressed and very turned on.

I can see straight through the facade she's throwing about though; I can tell she's scared shitless. Her eyes are wild, anyone who hasn't met her before would assume she was a crazy broad with a death wish. I had seen the same look in her eyes earlier in my office. I know she won't back down though. The stubborn lift of her chin and her *fuck you* body language dares anyone to challenge her. Backed into a corner this woman was a kitty with claws.

I liked this side of Miss Sussex; my dick was also appreciative of the display she was putting on. I seriously needed to throw some water on this situation.

"Excuse us for a minute Razor, me and Miss Sussex here need to have a word." I pull her away finding a secluded corner on the other side of the room, her back hits the wall with an "Oomph" and I place my hands either side of her trapping her in.

"What the fuck are you doing here Isla?" I growl.

Isla

What was I doing here?

Call it sheer stupidity, or the three shots of tequila I had thrown down when I got in here; it was amazing what a bit of alcohol did for your confidence. I had bitten off more than I could chew. I couldn't let those big burly men see my weakness even though my stomach was in knots. How dare they think it was acceptable to put their hands on a woman without her permission. I was terrified but I wouldn't back down. If there was anything that ground my gears it was lack of manners.

I thought I could meet Jamie here, maybe I could help in some way. He said there was someone here with information on the Cartel, surely if any information is available, I should be able to hear it with my own ears. I had expected him to be here sooner than this, the clientele here weren't my usual crowd, but I was adaptable. The outfit I decided on seemed to help me blend in, that was until that big Lummox decided to try and paw me.

Now, looking at Jamie's ticking jaw and angry glare aimed straight at me, as he cages me in with his big body, I realise that my entire plan for this evening had been one big mistake.

He is so pissed with me.

"I'll ask you one more time Isla what the fuck are you doing here?" He spits.

My temper builds at his tone, I never take kindly to being spoken to harshly by anyone I've had just about enough of these men thinking they can treat me like I am the weaker sex. "Don't you dare raise your voice at me Mr Conroy, I am a grown woman, if I want to go to a biker bar for a drink, that is exactly what I will do. And FYI your friend over there is a sexist pig and deserved the tongue lashing he just got from me. I don't take kindly to having my ass grabbed."

He looks at me quizzically for a second and then the jerk starts chuckling at my outburst; I'll be damned if it wasn't the sexiest thing I've ever heard, but I am not in the mood to be made fun of. I wrap my arms under my chest in defense and huff childishly. I was doing some glaring of my own now.

His eyes drift to my exposed cleavage through the tear in my shirt and darken, his laughter stops.

I push my chest up more enjoying his eyes on my bare skin. His gaze travels back to my eyes his eyebrows raise, I glare back challenging him, there's something primal in the way he's looking at me now. I suppress an urge to rub my thighs together to ease the heat starting between my legs, this man has me all kinds of hot and bothered, I can't seem to be able to switch it off.

His mouth is suddenly descending towards mine. *Is he going to kiss me?* I drop my arms and I lift my lips to meet his... He doesn't. He diverts his mouth last second to my ear, leaving me all kinds of confused and frustrated.

"That sexist pig you were giving hell to is my informant and a good friend of mine Sweetness. Now I'll let you tag along but, you must behave. Do you think you can keep those claws away for the rest of the evening Miss Sussex?" I nod unable to speak for the sensations cursing through me as his warm breath blows seductively against my ear with every word.

"Good girl, oh and FYI, I like this side of you–*feisty*. Now I'll introduce you properly to my good friend Razor, the Vice President of The Maw of Fenris Mc."

Fuck....

CHAPTER EIGHT

Jamie

We've been talking to Razor for the last forty-five minutes. It's as I suspected; Kevin is in deep. Razor informs us he's the Cartel accountant and general bitch boy and has been for the last four years, Razor confirms the lack of information on Mr Peterson before then.

Isla hasn't said much; I was expecting her to lose her shit but she's just sitting taking everything in. I can tell it's affecting her more than she's letting on, but she's holding it together surprisingly well considering.

"So, all the time he was away on business, he was with them?" She enquires, a calmness in her tone, too calm for my liking. I want her to get mad, she has every right to be pissed at the world right now, she's just found out her fiancé has lied to her for the last four years.

"Probably, the guys a manipulative weasel. I am sorry to be the one to tell you, but it's looking likely that him getting involved with you was his cover until the feds eased off and they could return to business as usual. Three weeks before you started dating, sixteen of their associates were arrested for intent to supply high class cocaine. The main heads in charge all disappeared. That picture you have is the first sighting of one of the main members of the Cartel in three and a half years. You need a good bookkeeper for money laundering Darlin and your Kevin as well as being handy with a blade is one of the best accountants the Cartel has ever had, you've been shacked up with a snake." Razors tone is soft as he talks.

We both watch the change in her beautiful face as reality dawns. Sharing a knowing look between us, this was the toughest part of missing person cases. Giving the family bad news normally consisted of "They don't want to be found" or "Unfortunately they died" not "Oh by the way your intended is actually a main contender in a huge drug ring." I never became attached I never felt anything other than sympathy for my clients, it was a job nothing more nothing less, handing out bad news came with the territory.

But, this felt different. Seeing the pain on her face was like a punch to my gut, I wanted to tear a new asshole in the man that had put that look on her face. After tonight I had to back off a bit before I became too emotionally involved. Business and pleasure never mixed well, and I knew if I got a taste of her it would be very pleasurable.

"So, is his name really Kevin? I mean I met

his sister and her husband; we were planning on getting married next year."

"I am certain Kevin was his cover, his family were probably other Cartel members playing an integral part. Jamie here will do some more digging to get a name for you." Razor replies his voice laced with empathy.

"I don't understand how I didn't know or even sense something was off. You must think I am pretty stupid huh? Getting myself in bed with the Cartels golden boy and not even realising." She laughs sarcastically shaking her head "I'm a darn idiot."

"You are not an idiot. This is what they do Isla, when the shit hits the fan the important members create new lives for themselves and build new identities until it blows over. They allow the lesser members to hold the fort until it's safe for them to make an appearance. You said yourself he was at business meetings a lot, did they become more frequent over the last year?" I ask cautiously.

She gnaws on her bottom lip. "He got a promotion last year which meant he had to go away for a week or two every couple of months. Realisation flashes in her eyes. "There was something– a few months ago he came home bloodied, angry and shaken up, he said him and his colleague had been mugged outside work. The strange thing was he had no bruising or cuts after he showered the blood off–when I questioned him he said all the blood had been from his friend. I didn't doubt him at the time because of how irritated he seemed, but there was an awful lot of blood, I had to throw away his suit and shirt."

"Can you remember what month it was Isla?" Razor queries frowning.

"It had to be around the end of January beginning of February. Why?"

"That was around the time they found those cops in the dumpsters downtown. The evil Fuckers chopped them into little pieces, it was like something out of a horror movie–the feds are nervous now, killing cops is a whole new ball game for the Cartel." Razor states. I give him a warning look to stop talking as I watch the color drain from Isla's face. Her bottom lip trembles.

"Oh, I remember that being all over the news at the time–I–er–please excuse me I need some air, this is a lot to process."

I am up out of my seat before she moves. "I'll take you home." I turn to my friend, "Razor, as usual thanks for your help buddy. I'll be in touch."

He stands and we clasp hands throwing in a manly hug slapping each other's back.

"No problem, stay safe JC. We're only a call away if you need us." Razor says quiet enough so only I can hear.

Things could start getting messy if the Cartel find out I am asking around about them, it was already bugging me that someone seemed to want me involved. I needed to do more digging and find out who sent that note with my details on.

"Nice to meet you Wild Cat, I hope we meet again." Razor smirks at Isla, who smiles shyly back and nods mumbling "Me too." She seems to have warmed to him now after their first meeting. Razor is a charming bastard when he wants to be.

I lead Isla out of the club and into the warm Los Angeles air. The parking lot is much quieter now, eerie. Something doesn't feel right. It could be my military paranoia kicking in though.

Suddenly, gunfire rings out in the air from our left, I throw Isla to the ground behind a truck shielding her petite body with mine. The only sound she makes is a whimper.

"Don't scream Isla, it'll draw attention to our location," I whisper as I lift my body off hers and peer through the window of the truck.

There is a man approaching his gun held steady, face unreadable in the dark but I can tell he's aware of our location. *Fuck.* I pull my Glock out and take the safety off, crouched and ready for what comes next.

"Send the bitch out, Nico wants his woman back. I promise no one will get hurt if you send her out now. If I have to come and get the bitch, you'll die slow."

Isla whimpers again beside me, her eyes wide with fear.

There's shouting from people coming out of the club to investigate, the gunfire has obviously drawn attention from the bikers inside. I risk a look through the window again, the gunman is distracted by the commotion coming from JoJo's. I creep out until he's in view and take my shot blowing a hole in the hand, he has the gun in. He bellows in agony dropping his weapon. Within seconds he is tackled to the floor by two of Razors prospects.

Isla is sitting knees pulled up, her hands covering her ears with her eyes tightly closed. I place my hand on her knee. Green tear-filled eyes open meeting mine so full of fear.

"Hey, you're safe beautiful, he can't get to you now," I sooth. She nods, her entire body shakes and she aggressively palms away renegade tears.

"You and the lady ok Bud?" Razors voice booms over the top of the truck. I stand and send a reassuring thumbs-up to him as I pull Isla to her feet and lead her to my car. I open the passenger door and ease her into the seat kneeling so I'm at eye level.

"Wait here and keep the doors locked, I'll sort this then I'll get you out of here ok?" I brush her hair away from her face. She nods again, her whole-body trembles and fresh tears stain her gorgeous cheeks. I grab her hand making her look at me. "You are doing amazingly well beautiful, so brave, not long and we'll be out of here I promise. He won't get you Isla, you're safe. You have my word."

"H–he said Nico who's Nico?" She stutters.

"I think that's Kevin's real name beautiful;

I'll find out, don't you worry about that right now. I just need to sort this out then we're out of here. Please stay in the car, I'll be back in a couple of minutes."

I lock the car and join Razor and his men who have the gunman's unconscious body by the scruff. His face is bloodied from where they've pummelled him a few times.

"What do you want us to do with this piece of shit Boss?" One of the prospects asks, he has the promise of murder in his eyes.

"Take him to the slaughterhouse for questioning, don't kill him though Gator, we need to find out what he knows," Razor orders.

"I hear ya. Tank, help us get this Fucker in the truck." Gator hollas to his buddy, kicking the body again. Gator and Tank load him in roughly and speed out of the parking lot.

"Get that lady out of here Conroy, I'll find out what that Fucker knows and be in touch."

"Nah, I want to be there, send me the address of the place you're holding him, I'll be there tomorrow around noon." I say abruptly, "I want in on this."

"I haven't seen you this fired up since Afghanistan. It's good man, you're gonna need that anger to face whatever's coming." Razor states. He's unable to hide the excitement. He always did prefer it when we were in the center of a battle, the sick bastard. "We'll hold him for you, can't promise he'll be in good health when you get there though, my boys are ruthless." Razor says chuckling.

"I don't care what state he's in as long as he can still talk," I reply sternly.

"I hear ya Bud. We better get out of here before the cops arrive. I'll be in touch. See ya later." Razor says heading over to the rest of his guys at the bikes. I walk to the car, unlock it, get in and start the engine. I glance over to Isla who is staring out of the window, her face ashen.

"You're going to stay with me until I know you're safe, my place is secure, and I can protect you there, I'll sort out a safe house for your family."

She doesn't argue, she doesn't even blink, she's in shock so it might be awhile before she snaps out of it and speaks again.

I pull out of the parking lot and take all the back roads to my apartment.

CHAPTER NINE

Isla

My whole body is shaking, and I can't get it to stop, I want to scream, cry or throw an all mighty tantrum for the way my life is heading, instead I stare aimlessly out of the window.

Shadowed buildings give us darkened cover in the backstreets of LA. Jamie said we had to keep watch to make sure no one was following us. I can't see anything. I blow out the breath I've been holding on to trying to calm my erratic heartbeat, it's useless. It doesn't help. Nothing helps...That's a big fat lie, Jamie helped. The touch of his hand in mine, that was the only thing that calmed me back at the parking lot. I don't know why but I feel safe and at peace around him, there's something about Jamie Conroy that puts me at ease.

I risk a peek at him. He's quiet, battling his own demons. He always looks like he's lost in his own thoughts, him and Razor were talking before about their time serving together, his time in the Marines must have been tough.

He looks so put together when he's in action though, like being shot at is normal to him. I suppose it is in his line of work. Serving in the military must make you hardened to the sound of gunfire and having a target on your head. He's was so brave. The way he covered me with his body when those gun shots went off, shielding me. Protecting me. I owe him my life. I shiver. What could have happened if he hadn't been there?

He catches me watching him, the corners of his mouth tilt in a small smile. I look away quickly butterflies dance in my stomach, the air is filled with tension. I try to suppress another shudder that wracks through me and fail miserably.

"We're nearly home beautiful, not much longer." his deep voice penetrates the air sending tingles through my whole body. I nod unable to talk; I can't even look at him in case he can see exactly what I am thinking.

Home? Beautiful? Did he really think I was beautiful? Or, was he just trying to sooth me, make me feel better after what we'd just been through? That wasn't the first time he had called me that...Whatever, it feels good.

Did he talk to his lovers like this all sexy and gruff with that deep growl of his as he made love to them? I imagine he's a talented lover...Now I was getting flustered thinking of his hands and mouth on my skin, I can feel my cheeks heating.

We turn into a guarded parking garage underneath a massive apartment complex. Jamie waves at the security guard as he pulls in and finds a space. He climbs out asking me to wait as he walks around opening my door and holding out his hand, I take it allowing him to pull me up.

It's cold, I shiver folding my arms around my body. Jamie removes his jacket and throws it over my shoulders, I meet his eyes and mouth my "Thank you" through chattering teeth.

His masculine scent surrounds me, I pull the coat closer filling my senses with his aroma. I begin to feel a little warmer as we make our way to the escalator, suddenly it dawns on me that I've only said two words to him since the club, I grab his arm to get his attention.

"Thank you, not just for the coat, but for saving my life tonight," I say surprised my voice sounds stronger than I expected. His eyes drift to my lips then back to my eyes. Is he contemplating kissing me? I want him to. Anticipation builds as I wait for his head to dip.

He pulls away and that wall is built back up between us as something unreadable flashes in his eyes.

"It's my job to look after my client's welfare Miss Sussex. Let's get, upstairs shall we. I have some phone calls to make. This way," he orders.

Just like that he's back to Mr P.I. I don't argue I just follow and try to hide my disappointment; it's probably for the best anyway, things are complicated enough.

Jamie

I nearly fucking kissed her, and she had wanted me too. *Shit.* What the hell was I doing? I had to get my head back in the game, but the look on her face, the undeniable attraction between us and the fact that both of our adrenaline is pumped after the night we've just experienced together... It is getting harder to resist tasting that perfect little pout of hers. I want nothing more than to give in and lose myself in her, but I know once wouldn't be enough.

Isla Sussex wasn't a booty call or a one night stand, she was a forever kind of girl and that scared me more than the bullets we had just dodged.

I watch her as she clings to my leather jacket like it's a security blanket, her mind is a million miles away.

We enter the escalator, the doors close imprisoning us together in the metal container. I notice Isla's grip on my jacket intensify, the furrow of her brow, the lowering of her shoulders as she tries to make herself smaller.

She has a fear of confined spaces?

"Hey, are you doing ok over there?" I ask softly. The shake of her head and the tremble vibrating through her tell me I am asking a stupid question; of course she's not ok and it's not just from being in this contraption; tonight had been a clusterfuck of a night.

I close the distance between us and pull her into my embrace, wrapping my arms securely around her. Her face is buried against my chest. The tremble in her body turns into sobs, her tears soak my t-shirt; I hold her until her sobs turn into tiny hiccups. I press the button for my floor keeping her close to me. She feels so good pressed against me, the scent of her familiar shampoo fills my nostrils, my mind spirals with all the things I would love to do with this beauty.

Her head lifts her eyes are swollen, cheeks tear stained and there's that hunger back, the look that tells me she's wondering what it would feel like with my cock buried deep inside her.

Even with smudged mascara and puffy eyes she's the most beautiful woman I've ever laid eyes on.

"Do you really think I'm beautiful?" She sighs, her words shake me slightly. *Did she just read my mind?*

"You're the most beautiful woman I've ever laid eyes on Isla, I would love nothing more than to kiss you like your gorgeous eyes are begging me too. But I'm not going to. You're scared, confused and hurting right now," I tell her honestly.

"I am scared, but I am certainly not confused. Me and Kevin, Nico or whatever his name is, are over; he got someone to come after me with a gun. I don't know what I am doing right now my head is a mess. But, I do know that I need to feel something. Something else."

Suddenly, she is on her tiptoes and her mouth is pressed against mine, warm, soft and perfect. My head turns fuzzy and I nearly give in to the moment; but before I can taste her like I want the reality of what she's doing hits her. Abruptly, she pulls out of my arms and stands on the other side of the escalator breathing heavy with her fingers pressed to her lips, looking mortified with herself.

"I am so sorry I did that," she whispers, embarrassed. *Fuck.*

The escalator comes to a stop, we stare at each other for a few seconds, the air is electric.

The doors open and I grab her hand and pull her in the direction of my apartment. She wants to be kissed so damn bad I'm going oblige. I am sick of holding back.

I open the door quickly and pull her inside. As soon as the door is slammed shut, I pull her close discarding my jacket from her shoulders to the nearest chair.

"Never be sorry for kissing me. *Ever.*" I growl pressing my mouth to hers eagerly, waiting for her to respond. I don't have long to wait as she moans sexily and opens up for me. Her tongue dances provocatively with mine, her hands work their way around my back and under my t-shirt, the feel of her hands on my bare skin drives me past the point of all reasoning, all I can think about is being buried deep inside her. My cock feels like it's trying to push out of my jeans. I can't stop the satisfied growl that leaves me as I drag my mouth away placing my head against hers.

"Isla. *Fuck*," I sigh frustrated. I need to stop this before it goes too far.

"Please Jamie. I need this–you." Her fingers trace the skin on my lower back, they brush against the scar tissue there, but she doesn't say anything about the raised skin she undoubtably feels, she just keeps on drawing lines on my sensitive skin. Other women always want an explanation about my scars. Not Isla. She gets it. I knew she would. She understands the battles we've both been through in our lives, battles that have lead us to this moment. Fate has brought us here and I am not about to waste a second of it.

I am about to break the only rule I've ever followed since taking over my Father's business.

CHAPTER TEN

Isla

T-shirt, boots and jeans leave my body in a frenzied rush to get naked. Jamie's mouth trails kisses across my stomach dipping lower until he reaches my black panties tearing them away from my body like paper, he thrusts into my sex with his rough tongue. *once...twice...three times oh...*My knees buckle at the sensations and I cry out.

"Delicious" Jamie growls standing and lifting me off my feet. I wrap my legs around his lean waist.

He carries me into his bedroom, never breaking contact with my lips until I feel my back hit soft sheets then his mouth is seeking out mine again, I can taste myself on him, it is the most sensuous thing I've ever experienced, I can't hold in the moans that escape.

My bra is gone and I am completely naked. He sits back on his heels, his eyes feast on my exposed flesh, he growls and his mouth is on mine again.

"Miss Sussex you are fucking perfect," he declares against my lips.

He moves off me, standing to remove his t-shirt and jeans. I am open and on display to him.

His cock is freed from his boxers, it stands proud and large. I run my eyes up and down his beautiful body greedily, trying to take a mental picture in case this is the only time I get to see him like this. He's gorgeous, all tanned skin and muscled abs. He looks like something out of magazine. The scars on his back just add to my attraction, I don't know how he got them, but I am certain it was something heroic, they make him seem more human, *just more.*

A wave of embarrassment comes over me and I suddenly feel self-conscious about being this exposed to another person. Kevin was never bothered about my needs and he certainly never made me feel like this. We rarely had sex naked and it was always quick. What if I am a disappointment? I sit up pulling my knees up to hide my body.

Jamie sits next to me, concern fills his handsome face. "Did I hurt you?" He asks placing his hand against my knee tenderly.

I hate that he thinks it's something he's done wrong. "I've only ever been with one other man and I–I felt different with him. He was never gentle, even when he knew I–I hadn't been with anyone else. With you it feels good, different, I just don't want to disappoint you," I tell him honestly.

Jamie's eyes soften, he gets it. This was a

new experience for me. Leaning in he captures my mouth with his and kisses me slow and so passionately, all the tension fades and I relax as he pushes me down gently against the sheets, trailing soft kisses across my cheeks and jawline making me whimper.

"You could never disappoint me and I will never hurt you beautiful girl, I just want to make you feel good, I want to hear you cry out my name as you come on my tongue."

I whimper again as he moves slowly down my body, each flick of his tongue on my sensitive skin sends new waves of need to my throbbing sex. I can't stop the little gasps that leave me as he explores my curves with his talented mouth drawing little circles on my skin.

He finally reaches my soaking wet center, opening me up, working slowly like he's savouring my taste. My back arches off the bed when he pushes a single finger inside of me, his tongue still working its own magic as his finger pumps in and out bringing me closer and closer to losing control.

The sensation is amazing and unexpected as my first climax hits hard, exploding against his tongue. My whole-body shudders as I come down, little currents of electricity still send shock waves through my pulsating sex. Jamie kisses his way up my body so he's hovering above me resting on his elbows. I can feel his hardness pressed against my inner thigh.

"Are you ok beautiful?" He asks kissing my neck, his voice strained.

"More than ok," I reply. He chuckles at my breathy answer.

"Well it gets better," he declares reaching for the foiled packet on his bedside table and tearing it with his teeth. He rolls the condom on and positions himself at my entrance.

"*Fuck*, Watching you come undone with my mouth on you is the hottest thing I've ever seen, Isla do you know what you do to me?"

"Show me," I reply lifting my pelvis so he can thrust into me deeply.

"*Fuck*. So perfect, so tight," he gasps filling me up.

There is a slight burning as he stretches. He stops allowing me to adjust to his size, his tortured eyes meet mine. "Are you ready for me beautiful?" His voice is strained. I reply by moving my hips again and he thrusts even deeper, we both lose ourselves in eachother. Every sensation feels unbelievable. Every nerve ending is tingling as his hips move slow and steady; it's like he's savouring each movement. My entire body is alive and humming with sensual gratification. I don't ever want this to end.

I run my nails down his back lightly and grip his ass hard meeting his thrusts, his hands move under my ass tilting my hips to change our position the sensation of his hands gripping my ass as he thrusts into me makes it so much more intense.

His cock hits the bundle of nerves deep inside and my walls convulse around him as another climax wracks through my body taking me by surprise, the intensity of my release has me moaning his name.

"*Fuck*, Isla, *fuck*. I can't hold on," he growls before succumbing to his own release. His movements slow as he rides out the end of his climax.

He kisses me passionately again, our bodies are still joined together. I can feel him growing inside me again. He is insatiable and I am unable to deny I want him just as much.

Jamie

We are under attack and currently regrouping in a derelict building, I can hear the gunfire a few blocks away from the rest of our Platoon. I have just been given orders to enter the red zone and unleash any force necessary to defuse the current threat. Razor is with me and Charlie one of the new recruits, everyone calls him Chomper because of his overbite, but he's a good kid with an impeccable aim and can handle a code red situation.

"Right, Chomper, head round the side of that building over there, dispose of any hostile you find, remember stealth is your friend and stay alert," I order. He leaves using the parked cars and trucks as cover. He

makes it to the building.

"Razor, we've got a coach load of kids to evacuate, the area is swarming with hostiles waiting to take their shot, be vigilant and stay safe."

Razor salutes with a wicked grin on his face and runs in the same direction as Chomper but has to lay low behind one of the trucks as the familiar sound of machine gunfire ricochet off the parked vehicles trying to shoot my friend.

I need to find a clear shot at that Fucker so we can get those kids to safety. My position from here isn't great, I need to get closer.

Keeping my rifle raised I run around the side of the building, I am constantly aware of my surroundings. There's a Taliban sniper on the roof of the building in front of me, he has his rifle trained on the other side of the street. I take aim and fire; I blow the top of his head clean off with a straight kill shot.

Happy there's no other threat for the moment, I move further around the building. The bus comes into view, it's filled with school children, the driver is slumped over the steering wheel dead. From what I can see he's been shot in the head.

I scour the vicinity, there's another sniper on the building across the street. His scope is trained on the bus, judging by the hole in the window screen I'd bet my money on that guy being the driver's assassin. As I aim my rifle a shot rings through the air and the guy I have my sight on is taken out followed by a "Can I get a whoop whoop" from Razor. I shake my head chuckling. He's a sick fucker.

I make for the building ahead of me rifle ready for action, I make it to the halfway point behind a parked car.

Gun fire rings out and I am in a standoff with three other men. I take the first one out no problem, the guy is erratic and can't shoot for shit. The other two have found themselves a good spot and I can't get a clear shot. I need to move, I run for the cover of the building managing to dodge the bullets fired.

I reload my rifle. Just as I am about to peek to take aim one of the fuckers tries to ambush me with an army blade, he's frantically swinging it at me like a man possessed. I am quicker. I disarm him taking the knife and slit his throat, throwing his lifeless corpse to the floor.

"Get to the bus Conroy I've got the fucker." Razor shouts as more gunfire fills the air.

I peek round the building at the carnage, Razor wasn't wrong, the other shooter is slumped against a wall opposite, blood seeping from a hole in his chest.

I carefully maneuver to the bus. I spot Chomper and Razor. Chomper is nearly to the doors of the bus. I don't like how easy that was. The street seems too quiet. Something doesn't feel right.

I am about fifty yards from the bus, innocent faces watch me with scared expressions, my focus is drawn to a dark eyed dark-haired little girl, her hand is press against the glass as she watches me. As I approach my eyes dart everywhere expecting more gunfire.

Suddenly, an explosion rips through the bus

tearing the metal apart. The blood curdling pain filled screams of children being burnt alive is the most horrific sound, I cry out in anguish my brain not quite comprehensive of what's happening for a split second.

I throw myself to the floor and cover my head, shards of metal tear through the back of my uniform and slash my skin open, it's pain like nothing I've ever felt before, I know my back is in a bad way, it cripples me just to move.

Determined to find someone alive I drag my battered body across the road, pushing through debris. My ears are ringing, the smell of burnt flesh fills my nostrils.

I reach the bus, pulling out disembodied limbs, ignoring the agony I feel with every movement. I know it's useless...I failed. They're all dead. I couldn't help them...

Hands are shaking me. Someone is calling my name. A woman's voice? That's impossible women never stay in my bed. Where am I? I try to push them away, I must still be dreaming. It takes me a moment to come around. I am disorientated and a little pissed that someone has witnessed my fucked up dreams. I don't have time to think anymore as my stomach convulses. I dive out of bed to my en-suite slamming the door behind me. I narrowly make it to the toilet bowl hurling my guts up. I retch and retch until my throat hurts.

I haven't dreamt of that day in such detail for a while. I lean my back against the cool wall and take a few deep breaths chanting my usual mantra of 'I survived.' 'I had no way of knowing there had been a suicide on that bus.'

No amount of therapy can stop the nightmares from recurring.

A light knocking on the door reminds me I'm not alone. *Fuck.*

"Jamie, are you ok? That was a pretty bad dream you were having." Isla's voice calls softly through the closed door. *Shit.* Isla is here, she stayed over, and I was supposed to be protecting her. This was exactly why I didn't sleep with women and usually kicked them out. What must she think?

"Leave me alone Isla." I snarl. I don't want her pity. I don't need anyone feeling sorry for me. I'm such an asshole.

I stand on shaking legs and lean on my sink looking at my reflection, *get it together Conroy.* I thought I was passed letting those dreams get the better of me, that one caught me off guard, maybe it was the excitement of earlier.

I swill my sweat soaked face with water. I turn looking at the scar tissue that covers my back, I focus at the one closest to my spine, 'Lucky to be alive' they said, but I hadn't known how close I had got to dying, that day. I had been driven by sheer adrenaline. It was only later laying in that hospital bed in agony and unable to move that reality had struck and the madness had clogged up my brain.

Razor had lost his leg and Chomper had half his face blown away, he had died a few days later through infection, at least I got away with my life eh? I snort at that notion.

Movement from outside the door snaps me back to reality and the fact that I am butt naked.

Only hours before I had been buried balls deep in that gorgeous woman out there and now, I was standing in my bathroom like a pussy telling her to leave me alone because I had a bad dream.

Seriously, get a fucking grip Conroy.

I rinse my mouth with mouthwash and walk back into the bedroom. Isla is sitting cross-legged on the bed wearing one of my t-shirts her hair is pulled into a messy bun at the top of her head, she looks beautiful. Isla sitting there in my clothes pulls at something territorial inside of me.

I thought she'd be mad as hell but the smile she gives me penetrates right to my soul. Her eyes go straight to my cock which is demonstrating how much he likes her too. I swallow, I'm feel-ing unusually vulnerable. She has just witnessed something no-one else has ever seen. What was it about this woman and her ability to break down the wall I had built in such a short space of time?

"Isla I'm sorry for getting angry before, I was an asshole." I tell her remorsefully.

She shifts off the bed and walks towards

me, the material of my black t-shirt barely covers her thighs.

"You don't have to be sorry; I know how it is with nightmares, I get them all the time. Do you want to talk about it?" She asks her voice husky.

"Not really, but I feel like I have to explain." She presses her finger to my lips.

"Well if you feel up to it you can explain tomorrow. I know something really terrible must have happened to you, I get it. I can see you have other things on your mind right now, and I am happy to take your mind off things for a little while," she purrs and lifts my t-shirt over her head, she's naked underneath. I reach for her, she comes into my arms willingly I lift her, and she wraps her legs around my waist.

I lay her on her back and bury myself inside her again enjoying the way her body fits so perfectly around mine.

I fuck her until we are both exhausted. Considering the night we have just been through and my fucking nightmare I strangely don't think I have been this relaxed in a long time. I lay awake with her wrapped around me, her head resting on my chest and her breath even as she sleeps soundly.

This woman seems intent on pulling down all the walls I have built around myself and think I am beginning to warm to the idea of letting her try.

Isla Sussex what are you doing to me?

86

CHAPTER ELEVEN

Jamie

I pull up at the Warehouse just after twelve, there's a truck and four bikes parked outside. I recognize Razors Harley immediately.

One of the prospects comes out as I approach lighting a joint and waving nonchalant.

"Conroy, the name's Tank I met you briefly last night," he mumbles offering his free hand, as he takes a long drag of his smoke with his other. I oblige shaking his huge hand firmly. This guy lives up to his name. He isn't very tall but what he lacks in height, he makes up for in width. He has a buzz cut that reminds me of my time in the military and he is covered in tattoos, my eyes are drawn to the tally marks on his left arm below his rolled up blue shirt currently shaking my hand, there's about ten visible, but I am certain there will be more higher up his arm, they were the markings of every man he's killed during his time with The Fenris, Razor has the same markings. I hadn't really paid him much attention last night in all the excitement, but this guy was a mean looking bastard.

"Has the fun began?" I ask amused nodding to the bruising on his knuckles.

His eyes light up, "Yeah it has, the pussy has shit and pissed himself, he should be good and co-operative for you," he says looking pleased with himself.

"Great, I don't intend on being here long, thanks Tank."

"See ya in a minute Conroy." I pat him on his huge shoulder and let myself in.

Tank wasn't joking, the smell hits me before I reach Razor and his gang, I am not a hundred percent convinced it's just the gunman's piss and shit I can smell. The scent of death also coats the air, rotten flesh and dried blood harness their own unique stench. I have numerous unpleasant scents imprinted up my nostrils. Unfortunately, I have a strong sense of smell, even the smallest amount could be detected by my nose, another perk of being Jamie fucking Conroy. The guys named me Bloodhound because I could pick up on different scents, like a certain type of cologne, a person's lack of hygiene or even the brand of liquor they drank. It was never a pleasant attribute to have, but it occasionally helped figure out what you were walking into during the middle of combat...The smell of death though, I don't think I'll ever get used to that, my stomach protests a little. Razor did call this place The Slaughterhouse and judging by the metal frames with hooks attached hanging from the ceiling I would say this used to be an abattoir before The Fenris took it over as their torture chamber.

It didn't surprise me, Razor was a 'say what you see' kind of guy; there was no sugar coating; he said what he meant whether you wanted to hear it or not. Despite the lack of filter, he was fiercely loyal and always had your back. Other than Greg, Razor was the closest thing I had to family left.

I enter another part of the Warehouse through some plastic sheeting. I hear Razors booming voice before I see him, he's cussing one of his men out.

I push open another metal door, my focus immediately drawn directly to the man strapped to a metal surgical table. Two of his fingers have been removed, both of his kneecaps are shattered, and his face is unrecognisable.

All eyes are on me as I enter, not all are friendly. I ignore some of the glares I get for my intrusion, they are protective of their Vice and their other brothers safety, I could be a threat.

"You guys certainly had some fun with this asshole," I say as I approach the six burly men dressed in their leather Maw of Fenris cuts.

Razor's laugh rumbles from his chest and he pats my back firmly nearly knocking the wind out of me, the heavy handed fucker.

"JC my bud. My boys are anything but shy when it comes to teaching a motherfucker a lesson," he chuckles.

I walk over to the table and lean over glaring directly into the assholes face.

"Are you ready to talk, or should I give the orders for these boys to have some more fun, I mean you've got eight more fingers and my friend here loves collecting toes." The guys eyes widen in fear and he nods. I remove his gag.

"Who's Nico?" I snarl.

"Nicholai Flores, he wants the woman back." That name, *fuck*, he a big player. Why didn't the nick name click before? I'm off my game.

"What does the woman have to do with the Cartel?" I demand.

"She's asking too many questions, she's got some big shot P.I looking for him called Conroy, Nico is worried he's trying to get info on the drugs they're trafficking across the border." He thinks I'm working for the MC he doesn't know who I am? "Conroy's old man was working against the Cartel and got himself killed a few years back, Nico had to go into hiding because the Feds got wind of his deals and came in all guns blazing. I swear that's all I know, I just had to bring in the girl."

My Dad was helping the Feds with the Cartel case when he was killed? How didn't I know this? I don't react, although every fiber of my being wants to know who killed my dad.

"Who does Nico have working for him in the Conroy building?" I snarl.

Razor frowns at my change in direction, a million questions on his face.

At least this asshole is beginning to look a

little rattled at my line of questioning.

"I don't know man, I don't know. Please. I've told you everything."

Whoever he was lying for had to be someone important.

"You're not being honest are you Fucker, I need a name," I roar, gripping the assholes face and squeezing hard; his good eye bulges from his skull.

"No please. I can't. I can't," he begs, the useless piece of shit. I let go and step back.

"Gator, take another finger!" Gators eyes light up at my request and he walks over with his meat clever.

"No. please. don't. Ok–ok. Roberto, that's the only name I have, I don't even know if that's his real name or if it's even a guy; they're a no-body, just the informant, it's someone close to Nico-I've told you everything.Please let me go, I promise I'll disappear. You'll get no more trouble from me Mr." An evil smirk tugs at the corners of my mouth, there was no way this dick was walking away with his life.

"I didn't introduce myself how rude of me, I'm Conroy, Jamie Conroy and Nico ain't getting shit. Razor make it quick," I say. I smirk again victoriously as I walk away. I can hear the guy screaming profanities in my direction before a gunshot sounds and there's silence.

I'd love to be able to say that I was remorseful, but in all honesty, it was another dickhead I wouldn't have to worry about later. The Cartel wanted a war, they fucking had one.

Isla

I pace the length of Jamie's apartment. Jamie has been gone for hours, my anxiety levels are through the roof. What could have happened to him? I pull out my mobile and try my Mums number, I needed to hear her voice; as much as she annoys me with her inability to cut the apron strings, I need her more than ever right now and she must be frantic with worry at being uprooted.

Why wasn't she answering? What was the blasted point of her having a phone if she never answered the damn thing? I hang up with more aggression than necessary. I take a few breaths, I am winding myself up for nothing.

Suddenly, the contraption in my hand starts ringing scaring me, I nearly drop the blasted thing. It's Jamie's number. I sigh a breath of relief.

"Hello," I say in my usual sing song answering a phone voice, although I have a good mind to cuss him out.

"Isla?" I nearly drop the phone again at the sound of Kevin's voice in the receiver. I don't answer. I hold my breath.

"Isla are you still there?" He sounds annoyed at my lack of response.

I do a little high-pitched squeak and nod my head like he can see my movements. Why can't

I speak? My whole body starts to involuntarily shake.

What was he doing on Jamie's phone?

"Listen baby." Baby? Baby? Was he for real? "I need you to pack a bag and come and meet me, you can't tell anyone where you are going, there's some bad people after me." He was obviously delusional, or thought I was. Now I was angry.

"You had someone threaten me with a gun last night Kevin, how can I trust anything you say?" I demand angrily.

"What are you talking about Buttercup? I would never do anything like that. Your friend Conroy found me, he told me I should call you from his phone and arrange to meet you somewhere. Please Isla, I've missed you so much. I promise if I could of I would have been in touch before now."

He's lying I know he is; Jamie wouldn't have done that without speaking to me first, would he? Or, maybe last night had meant more to me than him, I mean Jamie Conroy was an obvious bachelor who enjoyed playing the field. Had I just been played? Was this his way of getting rid of me without having to face me?

Maybe I could talk to Kevin, as long as we did it somewhere public. I had to do this sensibly; if he was telling the truth and he was now in danger and meeting with Jamie, Razor must have got it wrong about him being part of the Cartel.

He obviously thought something of me if he was so eager to get me back. Had I been wrong doubting him? I owed it to myself to tell him to his face that I was done with him. Even if things with Jamie were over before they started, the last few months have made me realise, I never really loved Kevin, I had become dependent on him, he was controlling and a jerk most of the time. We had become stale long before he disappeared.

"I'll meet you outside Starbucks, opposite Grand Park in an hour." I say quickly and hand up before I can talk myself out of it.

CHAPTER TWELVE

Jamie

"Who do you think it is?" Greg asks scowling at the screen at the employment files as I scan through their personal information.

"I don't know, but I am sure as hell going to find out," I spit tapping the keys on the keyboard a bit too hard, I need to take a break before I lose my shit.

I had to give Isla a call, make sure she knew not to leave the apartment. My gut twists. It is looking like they have used her to get to me; I swear if she get hurt there isn't a man alive who will stop me from tearing a hole in the bastard that dragged her into this. I grab my jacket off my desk and rummage through the pocket. My cell phone isn't there. I must have left it in the car.

"Can you scan through these names for me? I just need to go and grab my cell from the car." I ask, retrieving my car keys out of my jacket.

"Sure," Greg replies looking concerned as he takes a seat in front of my computer. He knows when I'm in this frame of mind it's better to just do as I ask.

"Thanks man, I'll only be a minute," I shout running out of the door to the stairs. The escalator is always busy this time of day and I don't want to make menial conversation.

I reach the lobby in minutes and power walk out of the door to my car avoiding the few employees who try to attract my attention.

I reach my beauty sitting in her usual spot, unlock her and pull open the door. I rummage around under the seats and in the glove compartment. My cell isn't here. *Fuck.* I know I had it in here earlier because I text Greg. *Fuck.* That was a few hours ago. It must have fallen out of my pocket in the building.

This day could go fuck itself.

I lock my car and jog back into the building stopping at reception. I check the blondes name tag at the front desk as I approach and grin widely.

"Hannah is it? I am wondering if anyone has handed in a cell phone in the last hour?" She blushes at my unexpected attention, and then smiles flirtatiously.

"Well good afternoon Mr Conroy," she purrs. I resist the urge to roll my eyes. "I haven't had any cell phones passed to me, but maybe my co-worker has; let me just check for you." She picks up the telephone on the desk and dials. The furrow of her brow and the disappointment on her face tells me what I need to know before she speaks.

"I am sorry Mr Conroy, no cell phones have been handed in today." *Fuck.*

"Thanks for your help, if one turns up can you get Julie to bring it to my office please?" I request, before heading across the lobby to the stairs.

"Jamie, hey." *Shit.* What the fuck is Lindsey doing here?

"What do you want?" I spit, annoyed at being stalked by this crazy bitch. I'm being rude, but she knows not to come to my workplace, I have more pressing matters to deal with, this was another giant ball ache I didn't need today. I run a frustrated hand through my hair and huff facing my former lover. She looks pissed as hell.

"Don't be an asshole Jamie, I just wondered where you've been? I text and called a few times and got worried when you didn't call me back, so I went to your apartment, there was some blond girl just leaving as I got there. When were you going to tell me, we are over?"

Did she say she saw Isla leaving? *Shit.* I need rid of this crazy bitch so I can get to Isla. My filter is now completely eviscerated.

"You were just a fuck, I was clear about our arrangement from the start, I thought you were cool with it, I was obviously mistaken. Listen, I haven't got time for this now Lindsey, I have to go," I growl brushing past her, ignoring the hurt look on her face. She was just a hook-up, I never lied to her, I was straight, she would have to get over it; Isla was my main priority and she was god knows where getting herself into trouble.

I had to call her, warn her about everything. I should have called her after I left the warehouse, but my dumb ass was focused on finding out who Nico had working in my building.

I sprint up the stairs taking two at a time. I am glad I keep myself in shape. I jog up to Harriet who looks startled by my sudden appearance at her desk.

"Harriet, get me Miss Sussex on her cell," I demand a little more harsh than I intend.

"Y-yes Mr Conroy," she stammers, not used to my abrupt tone towards her.

She finds the number on her laptop and dials handing me the receiver.

It rings and cuts to voicemail.

Isla

I'm beginning to get restless, I shift uncomfortably in my seat, I am too warm in my jeans and top from last night, but that's all I had with me, I've even had to go commando because I didn't have any clean panties; this sucks big time.

I just want to get this over with so I can move on with my life, I need to put all of this Kevin crap behind me. Just one coffee, a brief conversation and then I am out of here.

I huff loudly and pick at a loose hang nail making the skin bleed then inspect the damage. I really needed to stop picking my nails, they are ruined.

I glance out of the window, there's no sign of Kevin, Nico or whatever he's calling himself now. I look at the time on my cell and huff again. I've sat for the last hour and forty-five minutes. I take a sip of my latte; I push it aside. It really doesn't taste that great now it's cold.

I am leaving.

Kevin can go fuck himself and if Jamie has a problem with that he can go and fuck himself too. I leave the coffeeshop, the young good looking male barista waves to me as I walk out into the sickly hot LA air, I wave back enthusiastically, too enthusiastically for the way I am actually feeling right now, but my Momma taught me manners. 'Manners cost nothing' is what she used to tell us when we were little, her voice echoes in my head.

A bead of sweat trickles down my neck and into my cleavage, *darn.* I need another shower, a change of clothes and a large glass of wine, not necessarily in that order.

The heels of my shoes click against the sidewalk as I step to the kerb side to holla for a cab. I spot one straight away and stick my arm out waving to get his attention. Out of nowhere a black

Mercedes with blacked out windows cuts off the cab and parks right next to me. I want to cuss them out so bad. I don't have time to think as the passenger door opens, and I am dragged into the back seat.

I kick, scratch and scream for help but it's useless, he's so strong.

"Unless you want me to hurt you, I suggest you stop struggling Miss Sussex." His sinister tone promises a world of pain if I don't comply.

No, I won't be taken, I wrestle with the guy.

"For fucksake Franco, get that bitch under control!" The driver snarls.

I kick, bite and scream as the asshole tries to pin me down.

With a free hand I reach behind me into my bag, relief fills me when I feel my pepper spray, I pull it out and mercilessly coat my assailants face making him immediately grab his eyes and cough violently.

This is it, my one and only chance. I make my escape pushing open the door, the dickhead forgot to lock me in. I am out and I start running, I don't stop or look behind.

The roar of voices from my kidnappers as they yell profanities in my direction shake me to my core, my feet move faster creating distance between me and them. Escaping with my life is my only goal. I sprint across the sidewalk of Grand Avenue to the entrance of Grand Park.

The park is busy, and I am grateful for the first time today of the LA heat bringing this crowd out. I can finally slow to a fast walk, I glance warily behind, I can't see anyone chasing me now, thank God. I suck in some air trying to catch my breath, I grab my side to try and ease the stich I have developed.

I make my way down the steps which are covered in the most beautiful array of hanging willows and different colored plants. There are a few people sitting on the steps enjoying a lazy sunny afternoon.

I run down them and sprint across the park. I find a little secluded area with some seating; I can see the entrance to the park from here, I can't see anyone chasing me.

I think I got away.

After a little while, I dig through my bag to find my cell, my hands shake violently. There's a missed call from the Conroy building. I hit redial. My eyes dart everywhere.

"Jamie Conroy's office, Harriet speaking, how–"

"Harriet it's Isla–er Miss Sussex, is Jamie there?"

"Oh, it's you Miss Sussex." She sounds surprised. "I will put you through, Mr Conroy will be relieved." There's silence for a few seconds while she connects and I start pacing, my anxiety is at a colossal level.

"Isla? Where the fuck are you? I've been call-ing."

A sob escapes my throat at the sound of his panicked voice, I can't stop the tears.

"You tricked m–me, but I got away. You and Kevin won't–"

"Whoa Isla, what are you talking about? Me and Kevin? I haven't been with Kevin, I've been with Razor and then here at the office. I don't understand. Has someone hurt you?" He sounds genuine and really pissed at the thought that I might be hurt, but it could be a trick. Do I trust him or not?

"Kevin called me off your cell and wanted to meet me, his men tried to kidnap me. I–I got away." I hear him curse under his breath.

"Did they hurt you Isla?" His voice is laced with concern.

"I'm fine." I tell him my voice wobbles I am trying and failing to keep my tone hard.

"Isla, someone has stolen my cell, I've been going out of my mind since I found out you had left my apartment. We agreed you would sit tight until I got back, what were you thinking leaving the apartment alone Isla?" He blows out a calm-ing breath. "You're safe that's all that matters. I think this line is being monitored so I can't say much more." There's something in his voice that screams at me to believe him. Although I want to curse him out a little more, I know he's right about leaving the apartment alone, I should have stayed put, then I wouldn't be in this situation.

"Jamie, I'm so afraid, I don't know who I can trust anymore, not after today. I have never been so scared in my life." I whisper, wiping away tears that cascade like a waterfall down my face, my entire body vibrates with my sobs.

"Isla I swear you can trust me." He reassures. I might be going mad, but I do trust him, he about the only person I can trust right now and I need his help.

"Ok," is all I can hiccup.

"Listen, stay where you are, I'll get another cell and ring you back when I am in my car. I'm coming to get you."

"Please hurry," I mumble into the silence.

CHAPTER THIRTEEN

Jamie

I head towards Grand Park manoeuvring my way through the busy LA traffic, my adrenaline is pumping, I tap the steering wheel of my beauty, as the traffic comes to a standstill at some lights.

Razor is meeting me with a few of his MC guys, I called them after I got off my new cell with Isla. The way this fucking traffic is moving he'll definately be there before me.

Isla's safety is my main priority; especially now I know she is in more danger than we realised, Nico wants her back and god knows what he'll do to her if he gets her. Grabbing her in broad daylight was evidence of how desperate he was getting. My grip tightens on the steering wheel until my knuckles turn white; the thought of someone hurting her has me all kinds of fucked up.

Maybe I am being stupid letting Isla under my skin. Unfortunately, it's looking more likely we are both victims of the same piece of shit who had my father killed and he's using her as leverage. Who does that to someone as perfect as Isla?

A sadistic fuck, that's who. This whole shit heap could potentially blow up in my face and leave us both hurting in a way neither of us want, but I'll be damned if I was going to let that sick asshole have her. I've only known the woman for a few days but in this short time Miss Sussex has tilted the axis of my world and sent me completely off balance, I am completely out of my comfort zone for the first time in my life.

I don't enjoy feeling this unsteady on my feet. I am Jamie Fucking Conroy, I require control and organisation in every aspect of my life; I don't submit to anyone and I certainly never fall in love, love was for other people; love made you weak, it made you vulnerable, *fuck*, it gave the bad guys leverage.

No, I had to keep reminding myself that Isla is just another hook-up, a new plaything; I would grow tired of her once the novelty wore off, it always did with every female I take to my bed.

Who the fuck am I trying to kid? Myself? I snort at the notion.

I can't even convince myself she isn't already under my skin. Isla Sussex is magnetic, a glimmer of light in my darkened world. I can't remember having anything as fucking sweet, and if she's up for it we could carry on fooling around. We didn't have to commit to each other; I am not ready to let her go just yet.
But first, I've got to see what state she is in and be

grateful she's not tied to a chair or battered and broken somewhere. I swallow hard. Why does my stomach suddenly hollow out at the thought of losing her? "Get a grip Conroy!" I chastise myself as I mount the sidewalk outside Grand Park earning a few dirty looks from bystanders.

Razor and a few of his MC guys are waiting at the entrance for me. Razor greets me with his usual handshake followed by the obligatory slap on the back.

"Good to see you my friend, do we know her location?" Razor asks looking across the busy park.

"She should be hidden on the South-East side of the park, I've told her to be vigilant until we got here, she's a sitting target; even with all these people around Nico won't be afraid to take back what's his. I am not gonna let that happen." Razors frown deepens, his eyes narrow.

"You like this girl." It's not a question.

"That's irrelevant," I argue, wondering why he wants to talk about my feeling now when we've got a job to do.

"Oh believe me JC it's relevant, it's relevant enough for you to put yourself in the firing line for this broad. Believe me I get it; I understand protecting the things you love, but this isn't just a jealous ex it's the fucking Cartel."

"The Cartel killed my dad Razor. It's personal. Isla Sussex is just collateral damage. After this is over, we'll both get our lives back." I tell him not quite believing my words as they leave my mouth, neither does he.

"We'll see," is all Razor says as we head towards Isla's hiding spot.

Isla

My feet ache in these darn heeled boots, I'm tired and scared shitless.

I'm on edge; even the little old lady sitting on the park bench opposite is making me paranoid.

I peer across the park to the Grand Avenue entrance keeping myself hidden behind one of the many lush trees at the side of the steps. Jamie said he was on his way. I really wish he would hurry. I feel sick, the heat is sweltering and that old lady is seriously starting to freak me out with the way she's staring at me; I make eye contact with her, the toothless grin she sends my way does nothing to ease the tension in my stomach. She's probably just curious and I am just overthinking everything because of this messed up situation, I offer her a small smile back to be polite. I should move away from here before I attract any more unwanted attention.

I cautiously make my way out of my hiding spot and head for the steps, Jamie should be here soon.

I step out of the shade and spot Jamie and Razor by the entrance, for the first time today my tension lifts.

He came for me like he said he would, the anticipation of being back with Jamie has me feeling a little giddy. I start walking in their direction, my entire body is buzzing.

Suddenly, I am hauled backwards, a large hand captures my wrist, I lose my footing and fall scrapping the side of my knee on the concrete, the grip on my wrist tightens painfully as my captor bends to greet his victim.

Kevin's face comes close to mine, so close I can see the hazel ring around his iris and smell his familiar woodsy cologne. "Did you really think you could get away Buttercup?" He sneers using his usual nickname for me, a sinister air surrounds him. This is not the man I spent four years of my life with, this was someone else entirely. How was I so blind to this side of him? Why didn't I see what he really was?

Twisting my wrist in his grip only makes him squeeze harder, the pain that travels down my arm is excruciating, it takes everything inside of me not to cry out.

"K-Kevin, let me go, you're hurting me." I plead.

"This is nothing Isla, believe me when I say this is mild compared to what I am going to do to you. You had to come looking, didn't you? Desperation is an ugly thing Buttercup; you should have accepted I was done; I can't have you running your mouth off anymore, your drawing far too much attention to me."

A sharp stabbing pain radiates through my neck from behind, of course he wouldn't be alone, turning my head a familiar female face fills my peripheral vision.

"You," I slur. My body becomes heavy, the world becomes fuzzy, spinning and swirling. I am falling, falling down, darkness descends pulling me into the abyss.

CHAPTER FOURTEEN

Jamie

"Where the hell is she?" Someone asks as I search the area. I glare at the prospect who's looking dumbfounded, what a stupid fucking question, I don't even answer. If I knew where the hell she was I wouldn't have this feeling that everything was going to shit. My mind swirls with impending dread. She's not here, she promised she'd wait in this very spot. The fear in the pit of my stomach is growing with every second I don't find her. She's been taken, I know she has. I lose control of my senses, the familiar feeling pulls me into the darkness of my own thoughts. An involuntarily roar of frustration leaves me, as the reality hits me square in my solar plexus. Startled bystanders enjoying their afternoon walk through the park move quickly past me at my sudden outburst.

She's gone. I didn't get here on time. They're going to hurt her, punish her.

Visions of Isla with her throat cut fill my mind and I bellow her name. It's useless, she's long gone.

What they put their victims through is much worse than just a slit throat, she'll be tortured, raped and sold. My Isla...

I didn't keep her safe.

My hands shake, sweat beads on my top lip and I look to the sky searching for some kind of answer, the cloud of darkness is descending over me. There's blood on my hands so much blood. I fall to my knees. "Isla, I'm sorry." I am sinking, I know I am, I've let her down, I let everybody down...

I am back in Afghanistan the smell of burning flesh fills my nose blocking my throat, my chest feels tight and I wheeze, I can't breathe, I can't focus...big arms shake me violently.

"Conroy snap out of it man, don't you fucking dare clock off on me now. One of my men have just spotted Isla, Nico has her. They are heading towards the Civic center. Get your shit together soldier and let's go and save your girl." Razor's words pierce through the haze and I am back, the ground beneath me comes into focus, I rub my hands in the dirt to make sure it's real.

I haul my ass up, ignoring the urge to hurl my guts up as my head spins. Taking a few deep breaths to calm my protesting stomach, I meet Razor's gaze, he looks concerned but pissed, I nod and grab his shoulder affectionately, I can't form words, but he gets it, it's not the first time he's witnessed me go under and it probably won't be the last. Taking in some deep breaths helps to clear some of the fog.

I need to get her back.

I start sprinting, pulling my Glock from my waistband holster, Razor and two of his men follow closely behind as we weave through the terrified crowd, stampeding through the park as they try to escape the stray bullets flying.

"I've got three of my guys tailing them, they won't get away." I hear Razor say, I grunt my reply as my feet pound against the concrete.

Nico is mine.

I spot Razor's men straight away. Why have they stopped? I am about to give them hell, as I get closer I realise what the problem is.

Nico and five of his men have them in a stand-off. Isla's lifeless body lays in front of Nico, I stop and aim my Glock and fire hitting Nico in the chest, he goes down, but the lack of blood tells me he's vested. Razor aims his weapon and fires hitting one of Nico's men in between his eyes.

A shot rings through the air to my left, one of Razor's men falls onto his knees, blood pools on his chest, his eyes are lifeless as he hits the ground.

The sound of gun shots fill the air as more of Razor's men appear. Razor launches into battle.

"I'll be fine Conroy, get to your girl." Razor

commands as he fires more shots killing another two of Nico's men.

I look over to Nico, he has retreated taking Isla, her body hangs limp over his shoulder like a rag doll. He carries her roughly across the road, were there's a car waiting for them.

Nico is injured, it looks like one of the bikers got him with a nice leg shot and those ribs of his must be hurting.

"Nico!" I bellow, giving chase.

He doesn't turn until he is at the car, a sinister smile on his lips as his men drag Isla into the back seat, I lift my Glock and point it aiming for his head, I pull the trigger and he moves, I hit his shoulder and feel gratification when his screams fill the air, he's dragged into the car by his men before they speed away.

I sprint after them, determination and sheer adrenalin has my feet pounding against the concrete with everything I have. They won't get away, I can't let them take her.

My Dad used to say, 'If you want something bad enough you need to fight for it.' Well maybe the old bastard had been right. I want Isla, no scrap that, I need Isla and I was damned sure these motherfuckers weren't having her.

The busy LA traffic on the other hand, well that has a different plan for me today.

I don't see it coming until it's too late.

I only feel pain for a second as my body is slammed into and flung over the bonnet. I hit the hard ground my body rolls sending a new waves of pain through my battered limbs, I can hear screeching tires and Razor's deep voice calling my name, the blackness drags me under mercilessly.

CHAPTER FIFTEEN

Isla

I blink a couple of times and wince, the pounding in my head feels like my brain is trying to escape. My eyes strain to see anything in the pitch-black room.

The rope restraining my hands above my head have rubbed my skin raw, my arms ache from being held in the same position for god knows how long and to add to this shit situation I've got myself into, I've pissed myself. As days go, I would say this one can can't get much worse.

I can hear male voices coming from above me, my eyes begin to adjust and I peer into the darkness, I must be in a basement or a cellar of some kind, I move to try and find a more comfortable position, it's useless; the rope digs deeper into my skin and I hiss through my teeth as my skin burns.

A shadowy figure shifts in the darkness, I bite my lip to stop myself from screaming. My heart is racing so fast I am sure it's going to beat its way out of my chest.

"So, she finally rises from her slumber, you

talk in your sleep you know Buttercup, although I already knew that. It's been a very illuminating couple of hours listening to you mumble another man's name. It's a shame Jamie won't be joining us anytime soon, the car that took him out hopefully saved me a job." That voice. It's the voice I used to look forward to hearing everyday now it is one I fear, I cower away, every nerve ending alive with the need to escape.

What was he saying? Jamie was hurt. No, he couldn't be.

I am glad it's dark and my reaction is hidden from his view, I can't let him see how afraid I am. The cheerfulness in his voice peeks my anger, I guess I still have some fight left, I grit my teeth in his direction.

"Go fuck yourself Kevin or whatever it is you call yourself now," I snarl, impressed with how steady my voice is.

Suddenly, there's a shuffle of feet and a big hand wraps around my throat squeezing tightly and cutting off my air. I gasp for breath, his face comes so close to mine, he presses his nose into my cheek.

"The names Nico sweetheart and the only one around here getting fucked will be you, you'll be fucked, sold and fucked some more until this beautiful body of yours is broken and used up, then I'll personally buy you back at a bargain price and slit your whore throat for my own enjoyment." His tongue licks the side of my face, my stomach re-coils. "Mmm, you still taste as sweet as I remember."

His grip loosens on my throat and I gasp for air, tears stream down my cheeks as I wheeze and cough.

"One of my men will be down soon with a change of clothes for you, you try anything I'll bring your sister here and make you watch as I slice her up, understand Buttercup?"

"Wh—"

"Understand!?" He snaps

I nod.

"Good girl," he coos stroking my hair. The urge to move away from his touch is so strong. I know I have to let this play out as terrifying as it is. Something shifts in the air and his mouth descends on to mine, I am frozen with fear, he brushes his lips across my dry ones, its soft and gentle. I feel bile start to rise from my gut.

He grips my chin forcing me to meet his gaze; there's a glimmer of familiarity in his eyes, like he's recalling a fond memory of us.

I have so many fond memories of us together, I can't believe this is the same man who used to love me so passionately. I was so stupid and let him become my everything. Now I know it was all lies. Deceit. A smoke screen for his true nature all along. I was just a distraction. A naive little girl. The perfect plaything. Well ,not anymore. I hold his eyes my own stubbornness and pride won't let me back down no matter how afraid I am.

He releases my chin and he's moving away from me and towards the exit; opening the heavy looking iron door let's some light in, I use this opportunity to take in the brick walls of the dirty cellar. There's a metal framed bed on the far side of the room chains hang from the walls with more ropes attached, there's dried blood spattered on the walls and floor.

Were they planning on keeping me down here?

I can feel the anxiety creeping in. I don't want to die, but I can't stay down here. I tug against the ropes, breaking the skin on my wrists.

"Please don't leave me down here, please." I beg unashamedly. He knows how scared I am of confined spaces. Something flashes on his features, and then his eyes harden again.

"Do as I say and answer my questions truthfully and you'll live." Nico declares slamming the door behind him, leaving me alone.

I sob into the darkness.

△△△

The rattling of the door has my entire body

on high alert, I have been here for what feels like days. A few people have come and gone bringing me food and clothing, there's a toilet and wash basin down here that I've been able to use. They removed the ropes yesterday after I shouted my throat raw, my cheek still stings from the slap they gave me, I rub the tender area I am sure there's a bruise starting. At least I got some sleep-well, as much as I could in this filthy place.

"No, Nico said to bring her with us, he has some buyer after some nice pussy," one of the men upstairs shouts as his friend unlocks the door and enters, a predatory grin on his face as he sets his eyes on me.

He approaches leaving the door wide open. Is this my chance to get out of here? I can take him. He's not very tall, wiry and thin with a shaved head which only defines the hollow of his cheeks. He has a gun tucked into his pants.

If I hit him right I can knock him uncon-scious and take his gun, he won't expect me to ambush him, those self-defense classes my mum made me take might just come in handy.

He gets closer the hairs on my neck prickle, my whole body vibrates. I sit with my head raised watching him, any minute now, I'll charge him and knock him out, then I'll have his gun. At least if I fail and they kill me I'll be free from this wretched place; either way I am getting out of here.

I'll count to three and then I'll make my move, one, two... another man appears at the door looking frantic.

"Fredrico, we have company, we need you up here." Sounds of machine gun fire ring out from upstairs.

"I'll be back for you later bitch!" Fredrico sneers showing his yellow teeth.

"Can't wait!" I sneer back sarcastically. He huffs and casually strolls to the door, slamming it behind him.

I leap from my seated position and run to the door pressing my ear against the cold, hard, metal. There's lots of gunfire and shouting out there but it sounds like it's coming from another part of the house. I try the handle and it opens, my stomach does a little somersault. The stupid idiot forgot to lock the door behind him.

This is it, my one and only chance of getting out of here.

CHAPTER SIXTEEN

Jamie

"Mr Conroy, I would strongly recommend you stay in hospital for a few more days, the concussion and that wound on your arm is only going to be aggravated if you move before you're healed." I grunt my reply dragging my ass out of bed, I barely hear a word the doctor is saying, I am sick of sitting around. After receiving that call off Razor my only mission now was to get the fuck out of here.

Two days I have been stuck in this fucking place after that car hit me and knocked me out cold. Apparently, I was lucky I hadn't broken anything, although the pain shooting through my limbs with every movement doesn't make me feel very lucky, lucky would have been walking away and getting my fucking girl back, *fuck.*

I was a mass of nasty looking bruises and a headache that made me feel like chucking my guts up every five seconds *yeah,* lucky fucker.

Once this was done I needed a fucking vacation, preferably in a bed, naked with a blond goddess under me, that's if she wasn't dead already. I had to stay focused and positive, I can't sink, not now-Nico wouldn't kill her, he had gone to far too much trouble to get her back.

Razor said they had found Nico's holding house and he is adamant Isla is being kept there. Razors men were currently surrounding the place, firing warning shots. She better be unharmed and in one piece or all the hounds of hell wouldn't stop me from taking every single member out one by one.

I had seen first-hand the brutality of the injuries these fuckers could inflict, the thought of them even breathing the same air as her had me all kinds of messed up and more determined to get out of this fucking bed.

I pull my jeans on with my good arm, the movement stings like hell and my head pounds as I stand. I don't give a fuck about the pain while my girl is still out there. If shit was going down with Nico I wanted to be first in line to give that motherfucker the beat down he deserved.

"Mr Conroy-"

"No disrespect Doc, but I need you to keep the fuck out of my way if you know what's good for you." I snarl, earning an intake of breath from the nurse stood next to the nerdy looking doctor. The guy reminds me of Egon from The Ghostbusters, tall, wiry with messy blond hair and circular specks, the fear in his eyes tells me he's realised what I am capable of and backs off; I know how intimidating I can be when I am pissed.

No one argues or tries to stop me as I limp out of the room and down the corridor, my good arm holding onto my bruised ribs.

One of Razors men pulls up as I walk into the warm LA night air, gritting my teeth I climb into the passenger seat, perspiration gathers on my top lip and forehead as I fight against the pain radiating all over my body.

Razor's guy hands me a plastic pill box, I take it and throw him a questioning look.

"Trust me, those bad boys will sort you out, I took them after having a hole blown in my leg last year, I was back riding with the MC after a few days, they took the edge off; Razor calls them his magic pills." He hands me a bottle of whisky, this was typical fucking MC first aid.

What the hell, if I was dying today at least I would go happy.

I pop the lid unscrew the bottle and guzzle down two of the pills, the amber liquid burns as it goes down in the best kind of way. I place the bottle by my feet and put the pills in the glove compartment.

"Where's this place then?" I ask.

"It's an hour's drive from here, but don't worry I can do it in thirty-five," he chuckles. "They don't call me speedy for nothing."

I snort my amusement, I'm highly doubtful his nickname comes from how fast he can drive.

"Boss man says your girl is in that house, they're some nasty fuckers those Cartel and they're not even big league. I hope she's valuable to them, because if not you might be collecting just body parts when they've finished with her."

I grind my teeth and stare ahead, if this asshole was trying to get me pumped he was going the right way about it, and he wasn't finished.

"Mind you all the sweet pussy they collect is sold to the highest bidder, fucking sex trafficking is big bucks to the Cartel."

Did this Fucker ever stop flapping his jaw? The name speedy definitely came from the amphetamines he'd ingested, but the speed freak did have a point, Isla was high-class and would sell for top dollar, I had heard the stories of the women they bought and sold. I crack my knuckles, and glare out at the LA skyline, Speedy carries on filling me in on all of the illegal shit the Cartel are in control of.

△△△

We pull onto a dirt track half an hour later, I jump out as soon as the engine stops, my head is still throbbing, but it's not from the concussion, it's from listening to this asshole talk for the entire journey.

Other than a dull ache my pain is almost non-existent, those pills certainly worked a treat.

"The house is close, just cut through those trees there, bud," Speedy tells me, pointing to a pathway.

"Aren't you coming?" I ask confused.

"Nah, I am here in case we need a quick escape out of here," he answers, shrugging his shoulders as he lights a cigarette, taking a long drag. I decide it's better not to quiz him if I wanted to be out of here within the next millennium, the dude could seriously talk. I salute and wave before heading into the trees.

Isla

The door whines as I open it, it's that rusty metal kind of noise that reminds me of a prison door, which is ironic considering this has been my prison for the last few days. The steep concrete stairs leading to the building at the top of them seem daunting. I start to doubt if I can actually do this, I have to though no matter how scared I get, the alternative is so much worse. I take the steps one by one listening for any movement from above me. I can't stop the tremors in my legs with each step I take.

The shouting seems to be coming from

outside in another part of the building. This fills me with a little hope, and I take the steps a little faster.

I reach the top. I'm in a large kitchen. It's surprisingly clean, modern and homely with granite work surfaces and tiled walls. There are two doors, one leading into the house, the other looks like it could take me into a utility room.

I choose the latter, going into the house means I could be caught, and I have every intention of getting out of here.

My bare feet move silently over the heated flooring, the shouting and gunfire is growing more intense. I move swiftly around the central island slipping the largest, sharpest looking knife out of the knife block not quite sure what I am actually going to do with it when they all have guns.

I reach the door and slowly pull it open, blowing out my relief at finding the utility room and another door leading to the garden outside.

The shouting is louder out here though, but still far enough away to indicate they are around the other side of the house.

I creep to the back door and open it, welcoming the warm night air that fills my lungs, I gulp it in greedily.

A huge lawn with tall wired fences covers the entire area, behind the fence is thick with trees. I need to get to the fence and see if there's a gap big enough for me to fit through, then I can find a good place to hide amongst those trees, I've come too far to give up now. My stomach flips as I step out onto the porch staying close to the shadows.

CHAPTER SEVENTEEN

Jamie

I've got my sight locked. One touch of my trigger finger and this assholes brains will be decorating the walls.

I stay low, camouflaged by foliage. I indicate to Razor to cover my left as I keep my eye on the target...just like that I am back in the field, conditioned and always ready for combat. Kill or be killed; only this time there's someone I care about counting on me surviving long enough to get her out of here, I am damn certain I'll die trying if I have too.

On that lingering conclusion to the penultimate ending of my life, I pull the trigger on my M24 SWS blowing a hole through my targets skull, the range is close so his head explodes with the impact leaving brain matter coating the white wash.

"Nice shot Conroy," someone comments. I don't look around or acknowledge their approval, my head is in the battle, my sight set on my next target.

Suddenly, the area to our left is torn up, the house is lit up with the enemy's returned machine gun fire.

Razor start chuckling to himself, his laugh is deep and rich, my friend's amusement pulls at the corner of my own mouth, when I realise what's so funny.

"I think Razors lost his mind," one of the MC guys whisper from behind me, his tone is one of fear and disbelief at Razors obvious enjoyment of this situation. My smirk turns into a chuckle of my own.

"Nah, they're just firing their weapons the wrong way the incompetent dicks," I explain raising my rifle again and tearing another skull open. I turn to Razor, his eyes are full of wild excitement, he's really enjoying being back in action, not that I blame him, the adrenalin is such a rush, I have a little buzz in my veins being back behind a rifle.

"I need to get in there man, I am going to make my way around the back of the house and find a way through this fence, get your men to keep them distracted."

"Tiny go tell the others to start taking out as many as they can. Pip, Leo stick by me, we're gonna make sure these Fuckers know who they're dealing with. Jamie, I've got your back my friend, don't get yourself killed."

I hand my rifle over to Razor a knowing understanding passing between us, I grab the backpack full of essentials and pull my Glock out removing the safety, before making my way through the trees.

The branches snap beneath my boots, the scent of gunpowder fills the air as Razor and his men work on keeping Nico's men distracted.

I trail alongside the fence looking for any gaps. I reach a piece of fence covered by the thick overgrown bushes, I drop the backpack ignoring the painful stabbing pains that shoot through my body.

Retrieving the multi-plier, I start clipping the wires of the fence, my senses on high alert as I work.

The hole in the fence is finally big enough for me to squeeze through, I feel the sharp edges of the clipped wire tear at my flesh as I push my big frame through the gap.

Finally, on the other side I take a moment to assess the area. I can clearly see the back of the house, it's eerily quiet considering all the trouble going on at the front of the property; I don't like this.

A movement catches my eye on the back porch. *Fuck*. It's Isla, her eyes are wild and scan her surroundings, the moonlight casts a glow over her pale skin as she moves; she is about to make her escape across the lawn, I bask in the sight of her for a second; she is so beautiful and the best fucking thing I've set my eyes on for days.

Another movement to my left drags my attention away; two men appear at the side of the house, they are moving cautiously around the building, the bigger one of the two has a shotgun raised and ready; the urge to run and grab her is so strong, but I know if I draw attention to either of us we'll both be killed.

She doesn't see them and starts her descent down the steps of the porch. *Shit,* she'll be killed on sight.People talk about time standing still, this is that moment for me. I hold my breath and wait.

Isla

The air is warm, that sticky kind of warm, were all of your clothes weld themselves to your skin. Despite the thick air, I feel cold, the shivers that run through my body make even my lip quiver. I take the first step off the porch, two more steps and I'll be out in the open, a running target for them to capture, that's if they don't shoot me for giving them trouble. Anything is better than being locked in that cellar. I'll welcome death if it means I am free.

It's so quiet, too quiet apart from the gun fire on the other side of the house. I can't allow myself to get too complacent, I need to go now, anyone could come to check on me-once they see I am gone I'm sure as hell they will come looking for me.

It's just finding my nerve and running for

that fence. There are enough bushes I can hide in, maybe I can dig my way under the fence, it's an idea and appears to be the only rational option I've got at this moment in time *if* I have any chance of surviving-*What's that?* I can hear voices coming from my right.

"Let's check on that bitch like Nico asked. I might just rough her up a little. You seen her right? Is she worth a good fucking?"

"She's a fine piece of pussy alright, high-class and as sweet as fuck, bet she has a tight ass too, Nico is soft on this one though. I say we fuck that bitch raw then shoot her in the head, I'll tell him we caught her trying to escape."

That voice, it's Fredrico from earlier. My grip tightens on the handle of the blade, if I am going down, I'll make sure I fight back, the only thing they'll get to fuck is my dead corpse. I take a step back onto the porch and look around; I don't have much time. There's a bench and a small table with a few chairs scattered around it. I creep to the table and lower my body behind it making myself as small as possible.

Darn it, I forgot to close the cellar door, they are going to know I am missing as soon as they reach the top of the stairs, I'll only have seconds to make a run for it.

The voices are getting closer, this is it run or be raped. What has my life become?

Boots hit the first step making the wood

creak, my whole body flinches, I steady my breath the best I can. second step. I close my eyes and say a prayer I hope someone hears. Third step. I open my eyes, fear takes over and I hold my breath as the two shadows pass by me unaware I am hidden here. The door is opened and they both stomp through.

This is it. My one and only chance.

I move quickly and as quietly as I can. My bare feet carry me down the steps and onto the soft, freshly cut grass. I sprint faster than I've ever ran before, my senses on high alert.

I hear them shout and curse as they realise I'm gone, my feet somehow manage to run faster, the trees and fence are growing closer. *Just get to those trees Isla, come on, get to those trees*, I repeat over and over in my head as my feet pound against the soft ground.

"Stop!" Fredrico screams as they both give chase. "There's no way-out Missy, be a good girl, surrender and we won't mess up that pretty face of yours."

I stop and turn, my breath ragged as I suck air into my lungs, my adrenaline takes over. I grip the handle of the knife so tight my knuckles are white, I point it threateningly at them both as they approach me.

"T-touch me and I'll cut you," I threaten breathlessly, spitting venom.

Fredrico starts laughing. "You hear that Antonio? She's going to cut us." Antonio steps even closer and my breath hitches.

"This bitch ain't cutting no one, I'll blow her brains out all over Nico's lawn. You hear that bitch? That little blade ain't nothing compared to my gun here."
Antonio mocks.

"Fuck you. You touch me I'll cut your fucking dick off!" I scream stubbornly. Let them shoot me, I don't care anymore, they'll have to answer to Nico once I'm dead.

"Have it your way whore," Antonio sneers and points the barrel of the shot gun at me.

They say life flashes before your eyes in the seconds before you die. All I feel is numb, and then disbelief as a single shot is fired from the trees behind me and a hole appears in Antonio's skull before he has a chance to pull the trigger; his body falls to the floor, blood darkens the grass around his head.

The look of shock on Fredrico's face is a look not dissimilar to my own, but for entirety different reasons.

I know it's him, I turn not quite believing it's real.

CHAPTER EIGHTEEN

Jamie

Her eyes bore into mine, the air is heavy with tension.

"You're alive." It's more of an acknowledgment than a question, like she's convincing herself I'm actually here.

"I am, I've come to get you out of here Isla." I tell her softly but I don't take my eyes off the asshole standing just metres from her, my gun aimed at his head; his eyes keep flicking in the direction of his dead friend's shotgun.

"I wouldn't attempt it if I where you Shithead," I warn him. At least the dick has the gall to look nervous. "Where's your boss hiding? I need a word."

He spits on the ground in defiance and gives me the stink eye. I'm torn between ending this guy or taking him with us for information.

"Nico's not here. They were about to take me to him when you showed up," Isla tells me. Her beautiful features are tired and there's fresh bruising on her cheek. "Th-they were going to sell me for sex."

She turns on Nico's man her face screwed up in anger. "These two pieces of shit were planning on raping me just now, weren't you?" He gives her a predatory grin. Even held at gun point this guy couldn't hide the fact that he was a sick fucker.

"We wanted to see what was so special about the 'Little Princess' in the cellar, you must have a sweet pussy for Nico to have gone so soft," he sneers at
her and her features turn to disgust

"Talk about my pussy again you filthy pig and I'll slit your throat!" Isla spits with purpose, pointing the knife in his direction. I am impressed, she really did have claws when she was pushed. The way her hand trembles though I can tell she's terrified and so could this fucker. The asshole looks amused at her threat.

"Go for it bitch, Nico will do a lot worse to me when he realises you're not in your cell," he taunts. Suddenly, he lunges towards her taking us both by suprise, time seems to slow down as I pull the trigger. I fire shooting him between the eyes, his body lands at Isla's feet.

I am expecting her to scream or do some other girly shit, instead she swings her foot back and kicks the fucker hard.

"You're not raping anyone now asshole, I hope you rot in hell," she snarls kicking the corpse one more time. She drops the kitchen knife and turns towards me her eyes glazed over with unshed tears. "Can you take me home?" She asks, her features are hard and emotionless.

"Let's get out of here," I suggest holding out my free hand, aware of the gunfire still going on around us, she walks over and entwines our finger, looking down at them for a second.

"Climb through that fence and then I'll carry you, your feet will be cut to shit walking through there."

She releases my hand and walks towards the fence climbing through, her eyes meet mine, something flashes in them, relief maybe, this little tiger wasn't letting this break her. Thank God I got here when I did.

"I'm glad you're not dead Jamie." Her admission and the steadiness in her tone catches me off guard.

"You and me both Beautiful." I reply, following her into the forest a little thrown at how well she is handling this situation.

Little Miss Sussex was full of surprises.

Isla

Jeez, this guy could talk. He hadn't stopped talking for thirty minutes straight, I mean I like to talk but-

"So where you from Girlie? You're a Louisiana girl ain't ya? I can tell a Southern accent when I hear one. I have-"

I switch off, his lips are moving but I've stopped paying attention, he's throwing questions about but keeps on answering for me, I'm tired of nodding at him. I look to my right, Jamie is staring off in his own world his lips are set in a firm line the muscle in his sexy jawline ticks occasionally. Is he in pain? Did he leave his hospital bed to come and save me?

I put my hand on top of his, to try and pull him from his troubled thoughts.

"Hey handsome," I whisper. Dark eyes meet mine so full of emotion; I have a feeling I am seeing a part of Jamie Conroy no one else has, I give him a reassuring smile letting him know I'm here for him.

"Hey," he mouths returning my smile, he entwines our fingers pulling the back of my hand to his lips before resting it on his thigh. We don't need to talk, not yet anyway, conversations and decisions can wait until later; knowing we're both ok is all that matters for now.

I watch the road, absorbing the last few days. Things could have been so much worse, that is the thought which keeps me from breaking down and letting this whole thing consume me. I try and process everything I saw and heard over the last few days.

I recall something Fredrico said earlier on

that field.

Nico has gone soft? Did that mean he had changed his mind about selling me? Maybe I was worth more to him alive? Does that mean he still has feelings for me?

I shudder as thoughts of him kissing me in that cellar flash through my head. I can still feel the roughness of his stubble on my cheek, see the coldness in his eyes. When Nico was pretending to be Kevin his feelings had seemed so real, I know I had grown to love him over time. At first he hadn't set my world on fire or given me butterflies but he had seemed sweet, gentlemanly and eager to get to know me. I now know what had developed between us was all lies and he was an evil, sadistic murderer. He had played me like the naive idiot I used to be. But, what if his feelings had grown too? We spent four years together, there were a lot of happy times. All of it couldn't have been fake, could it?

As if sensing my train of dark thoughts, Jamies hand squeezes mine gently bringing me back to the present.

CHAPTER NINETEEN

Jamie

Isla's whimpers of pleasure as I ease my aching cock into her tightness makes my eyes roll back in my head. The walls of her sex grip me mercilessly and I thrust into her wetness again slowly.

"So fucking tight, so fucking good." I rasp, as I move again making us both moan with pleasure.

It has never felt this intense. No other woman has ever had me this close to exploding inside her so quick, I have to take this slow, I want to savour every inch of her beautiful body, imprint myself on her so no other man will ever make her feel as good as I can.

Isla's hands grip my ass, her nails dig into my skin in the most delicious way as she pleads for me to go faster and harder. I thrust into her again slowly and she cries out in pleasure.

As much as I would love to plough into her sweet pussy and give her exactly what she wants, I am determined to make this last, I want to hear her scream my name as she comes, I want to feel her tight walls contract and the shudders of her release course through her, as she gives me all she has. I want to own her body and soul.

I shift our positions so she's on top, her gorgeous full tits bounce as she rides me slow, her eyes hooded, her kiss swollen lips slightly parted in ecstasy.

Cupping both of her luscious mounds in my hands I roll her nipples in my fingers earning another moan of pleasure from her, louder this time, her sex clenches making my balls tighten. I do it again and again, her breathing turns into moans with every thrust of our hips, I can feel her squeezing me, she's so close and I'm about to explode.

"Come for me Isla."

"Jamie I-" she pants as her orgasm rips through her, pulling me along with her as the walls of her sweet center contract, milking me of all I have, I unashamedly cry out her name our bodies in unison as wave upon wave of pleasure courses through us.

I'll never grow tired of feeling her surround me.

Isla

"Mum, I'm fine honestly, please don't cry."

"But I thought-" My mum wails, not finishing her sentence.

Lord give me strength to deal with my mother

when she's like this. I mean I love her dearly but sometimes, her emotions get the better of her and this is the shit I have to contend with. She has always been emotional, but since we lost my dad she has become so much worse. Sometimes it feels like I am suffocated by her. I understand why, I empathise I really do, seeing your child check out on life and cause herself harm, must have been awful for her-especially after losing my dad so tragically. I don't like to think about things too much, dredging up the past opens up old wounds. Life goes on right? I sigh as I listen to her tell me how I need to make sure I'm eating properly and taking my supplements. Consoling my mother for an hour wasn't on my to do list today, not when I have so much other shit to think about. But here we are, she is distraught and convinced I am lying to her; I am, but I would never admit that to her. The least she knows about everything the better. As far as she's concerned I am helping Mr Conroy with his investigation and in no danger. Imagine what she would be like if she knew I had been kidnapped, nearly raped and shot at; I shudder involuntarily, thank God for Jamie and Razor.

The real answer was no. No, I wasn't ok. I was scared shitless of what came next and doing my best to hold it all together.

Nico still hadn't been caught. *Shit,* I have to tell Jamie about the woman Nico had with him. We hadn't done much talking last night. I look at the unkept sheets on Jamie's bed my cheeks grow warmer.

"Mum, I'll have to ring you back, I promise I'm alright, this will all be over soon. I'll come and see you later." My promise of a visit seems to appease her slightly and I am relieved to hang up after a lengthy goodbye. I blow out a long frustrated breath.

"You're lucky to have someone to worry about you." Jamie observes from the doorway. His voice fills the room taking me by surprise a warm smile pulls at his lips, "sorry I wasn't listening in, I just came to see if you were hungry."

He's bare chested and wearing sweat pants low on his hips, my eyes travel from the light pattern of hair at his chest, down his delicious six-pack to the V which disappears like a sexy arrow pointing to the best prize of all. I lose concentration for a second as I feast my eyes on his impressive body, he's all ripples and tanned male hotness.

"Enjoying the view?" He jokes pulling me out of my perv-daze; I feel my cheeks heating again.

"Um-er, yes, you're distracting me. I have something to tell you about the day Nico grabbed me. I still can't get used to calling him Nico though-"

"Isla, you're rambling and pretty damn cute. Should I put a t-shirt on so you can tell me your news?" Amusement dances across his features, my blush only intensifies as I nod afraid I might start rambling again if I start talking, then I shake my head.

"Damn you Jamie Conroy and your ability to leave me mute." I sigh and he chuckles.

He walks over and brushes his lips across mine, his big hands on my hips cause all kinds of stirring in my lady parts, he presses his forehead against mine.

"You're pretty distracting yourself Miss Sussex." He admits. "Now, what did you need to tell me?"

"He had a woman with him," I explain. "I know her, her name's Joanna, we've worked together a few times on modelling projects over the years, I thought she was a close friend; in fact, she came to my engagement party. Why would she be working with him?"

"Have you got a picture of her?" Jamie asks frowning.

"Yes, I have, just give me a second." I say downloading some apps on my new phone. I open Google photos and log in scrolling through until I find the pictures of the Milan photoshoot I worked on with Joanna eight months ago. I enlarge the selfie of us grinning wearing our favourite dresses of the weekend.

Recognition passes across Jamie's face. "Fucking Lindsey!" He curses running his hand through his hair.

"Do you know her?" I ask, studying Jamie's features.

"She's a recent fling, I should have known

there was something off when she turned up at my work the day you were taken."

A fling, recent, jealousy builds inside me at the thought of him with someone else, but I push it down. My stupid insecurities had no business surfacing now. I knew Jamie was a playboy, I had no right to question him. I've been royally played, we both have; I feel so stupid. Tears burn my eyes, I blink rapidly to try and stop them escaping.

"Hey, Isla look at me." I can't he'll read every ridiculous thought. I have no right to feel like this, Jamie didn't belong to me, he was single, gorgeous and could have any woman he wanted.

"Isla, she was just another notch, and since the night you walked into Rocco's and turned my world upside-down no other woman has turned my head, please don't close down on me Beautiful." I meet his eyes, I see honesty and vulnerability, with that one look all my doubts evaporate. "We've both been played in this Isla, but at least it meant we got to meet eachother, in this big shit heap of a situation and whatever happens next, I will always be thankful for that." His mouth brushes against mine so gently and I wrap my arms around his neck returning his kiss. he releases my lips and rests his forehead against mine. "As much as I would love to get you back under those covers and fuck you until we both forget everything-we need to find out what her connection is to Nico."

Yes we do and when I get my hands on that

bitch she's going down, time to start toughening up and playing these assholes at their own game.

"I think I might have an idea where he kept his documents, but we're going to have to go to my apartment."

CHAPTER TWENTY

Isla

My apartment is just as I left it. There's a cold cup of coffee on the table in my lounge; it looks like the brown liquid has developed a new life form on the top of it. I turn my nose up and send Jamie an apologetic smile as I dispose of the contents down my sink, rinsing the mug under the tap. His expression is unwavering, the set of his lips drawn into a straight line. His mood has been hard to read all morning, I decide not to pry, we've both had a pretty shit week.

The reality of how low I had sunk after Kevin left hits me like a tsunami as I walk around, dishes unwashed, clothes thrown everywhere and God only knows what that smell is, *yuk*.

I tread cautiously into my bedroom already disgusted in myself and take in the unkempt disaster. This would normally be a time I cuss myself out but I am aware of the brooding hotness walking around behind me, so on this occasion I reel in my need to shout at myself out loud.

To be fair though my life had been put on hold for months while I was pining for a man who had been deceiving me in the worse possible way, so a dirty house is mild to what could have become of me; thank God I am stronger now.

I feel Jamie behind me as he looks round the room, he doesn't seem fazed about the shit heap I've left this place in. I however feel so embarrassed, this really wasn't me, seeing this now pissed me off at how naive I had been about everything. I had put my family through hell and turned into the worst version of myself, I owed them the biggest apology.

"Where did your fiancé keep all of his personal documents?" There's a business-like tone to Jamie's voice now all the warmth is gone; the smooth talking, tentative gentleman who had me wrapped in his arms less than two hours ago has been forgotten replaced by hardness. When I turn to face him, I am met with a stony expression, the tension is radiating off him. I consider having it out with him, not one to hold my tongue but I think better of it.

"There's a safe in the walk-in wardrobe hidden behind the suits, he said it was for all of his clients details, I was never allowed the combination."

Jamie pulls open the door and walks into the decent sized space, all of Kevin's clothes still hang perfectly neat, just how he liked them. That was another thing that used to piss me off about him, how pristine he always had to be, not a hair or cufflink out of place, he had been far too put together.

Jamie removes the suit bags covering the safe and drops them on the floor roughly. I can't suppress the fulfillment I get from watching the expensive material crease, I should have done this myself sooner. Jamie's expression doesn't waiver though.

The stiffness in his shoulders is evidence enough that he doesn't want or enjoy being here, you can cut the atmosphere in the room. I wasn't particularly having the time of my life either, this place had never felt like a home, not really.

He glares at me over his shoulder, angry eyes bore into mine. "You could have mentioned the safe before now, it could have saved us so much trouble." He snaps, my eyes widen in outrage at his hostile tone. He's choosing this moment to start an arguement? I lose it with him.

"Well funnily enough, I wasn't in my right mind for months. My fiancé had disappeared without a trace and then I was being shot at and kidnapped so the fucking safe slipped my mind ok? I would appreciate it if you didn't take that tone with me."

I storm out, slamming the door muttering "Asshole" as I go, I need to calm down before I throw something at him. I walk straight out of my bedroom to my lounge heading for the kitchen.

I run straight into Joanna holding a gun, pointed straight at my head.

Jamie

I am being an asshole, I know I am, but I can't seem to help myself, the thought of her living here playing house with that sick fucker knots my stomach. Seeing the pain on her face as she walked around her apartment reliving her life before had me all kinds of pissed.

Plus, I got a text off Greg earlier, Harriet hasn't turned up for work this morning and isn't answering her phone, so that means I'll have to go into the office today, which wasn't in my plans.

I am taking my shit mood out on the person closest to me, unfortunately that person is Isla. I can't seem to lighten my mood, something is niggling away at me, with all the shit happening at the moment I wasn't sure if my radar was off. I am beginning to question everything.

This was exactly why me and relationships never worked out, I was a bastard and everyone around me felt the brunt of my piss-poor mood. Of course she hadn't been in her right mind, I remember how fragile she was at our first meeting.

I need to apologize and then get this safe open, I just hope Nico hasn't been back here, I've had surveillance on the place but I wouldn't put anything passed the Cartel after all the shit I've uncovered lately.

I head towards the door, she's probably stomping around somewhere cussing me out, my little Southern Belle had sharp teeth when riled up, the more I got to know her the more I liked.

"Isla," I call stepping into her bedroom. She must be in another part of the apartment. "Isla, I need to apolo-"

Isla, is standing in the middle of her lounge eyes wide, her face a white as a sheet. Lindsey is right behind her a gun jammed into her side; big brown eyes glare straight at me.

"What the fuck are you doing Lindsey?" I growl.

"Taking Nico his whore back," she sneers. "He's grown soft on this one, God knows why, she's weak and pathetic."

"Fuck you bitch!" Isla spits. Lindsey digs the gun harder into her side making her wince.

"Who are you?" I grit out.

A slow sadistic smirk pulls at her lips. "It's not me you should be worried about handsome."

"Jamie, look out-" Isla cries her eyes pinned on someone behind me. Something hard hits me in the shoulder as I move at Isla's warning, avoiding a blow to my skull.

I whip my body round and come face to face with my secretary, her eyes are wild.

"Harriet what the fuck?"

"Surprise!" Lindsey cackles.

"We just want her," Harriet snarls, a look of hatred in her eyes I have never seen before and it's directed straight at Isla.

"You've been the informant all along?" I ask

dumbfounded, how didn't I know, background checks were carried out on all of my staff.

"Nico gets what he wants." There's a flash of pain in her eyes, which quickly turns back into contempt. "Why would you suspect the eye candy sitting pretty at the desk Mr Conroy hey? Besides, you should be thanking me, without me you would never have met Miss Sussex here...You're welcome by the way, I saw the way your eyes lit that day in the office, I knew we had you then, so fucking predictable."

Was she fucking serious?

"Why?" Isla cries. "What the fuck did I ever do to you?"

Harriet looks guilty, but then seems to gather herself again. "Nico promised me we would be together once he got back, four fucking years I waited for him, keeping an eye on his affairs while he played house; and what did he do? He fucking chose you." Bitterness laces her voice. "I knew once I got Conroy Investigations involved, he would have to sit up and take notice, I thought he would have killed you for contacting the man whose father had single handily tried to bring down the Cartel, but no, he just got jealous," she laughs humorlessly. "It worked out better than I planned when you two started fucking for real."

"You fucking sick bitch!" Isla spits. "Tell Nico-Kevin or whatever else he's calling himself, that I am not in the market for murdering scumbags, or to be used as a pawn in his twisted game. You're fucking welcome to him."

Lindsey laughs hysterically then, pressing the gun further into Isla's side tugging her hair pulling her head back, her mouth pressed against Isla's ear. She glares right at me. "Oh believe me Buttercup, you'll soon be singing another tune once my brother has you back and Mr fuck em an chuck em here is dead."

Brother, Fuck

CHAPTER TWENTY-ONE

Isla

Why am I not surprised Nico couldn't keep up his pretense without having help from somewhere else or at least another set of eyes watching my every move, but his sister *shit*; talk about keeping it in the family.

The desperation in Harriet's eyes tells me she has her own agenda and it isn't seeing me and Nico reunited, not that I would ever go anywhere near that psychopath again anyway. I have to try something to defuse this fucked up situation before someone gets killed. I know from experience of the bond between siblings and the fierce loyalty that goes along with it, the fondness in Joanna's voice when she talks about her brother tells me she's the younger sibling. I know exactly what it's like to look up to a big sister, always trying to gain their approval. I wonder if she feels the same about her sadistic brother? I decide to put my theory of loyalty to the test, I turn my attention to the woman who currently has my hair in a vice like grip.

"Joanna? Is that even your name or is it Lindsey?" I ask trying to keep my voice low. "I was looking for Kevin for four months, I thought he was dead; ask anyone how devastated I was. I loved your brother. I was going to be his wife, that has to count for something right? I had given up hope, then I received that photo of him laughing and smiling with someone who I now know is Marcus, it was like a punch in my heart knowing he had been alive all this time."

Her grip loosens on my hair giving my scalp reprieve from the tug of war with my follicles.

"What photo?" Her voice waivers. She doesn't know everything her brother's whore has been up to, my suspicions are right.

"He was sitting in a car with him, they were laughing about something. It was in the same envelope I got with Conroy's name on."

Her hand with the gun suddenly whips up towards Harriet, and I am cast aside.

"You fucking involved Marcus in this?" She spits at Harriet, who now points her weapon in our direction returning the threat. So it's Marcus she's loyal to not her brother, I didn't see that coming.

"Come on Sofia, you know Nico shouldn't be taking orders from Marcus, he's built up his own following now. This bitch here was just in the way, getting Conroy involved was a way of killing two birds," she admits. Jamie snorts a "Yeah right" but the two women don't bat so much as an eye lash in his direction. My eyes meet Jamie's and he gives me a look I can't quite read.

"Do you know what you have done? You have condemned us all. Once Marcus finds out his name is being mentioned in this fuck-up he'll have us all killed for sure. You know he wasn't happy about having to clean up the last shit heap you and my brother caused. I only got involved to make sure Nico didn't get himself into more trouble, and you, you have been stirring shit-up."

Harriet looks pissed. "Nico knows. We've been in on this together from the beginning, Marcus Ravenstone 's days of ordering Nico about are about to be cut short."

"Fuck you and fuck my stupid brother!" Sofia screams and pulls the trigger.

Time stands still as the gun next to my head is fired. I dive to the ground trying to avoid any stray bullets and crawl across the floor, not standing until I reach my hallway. I open the front door and escape down the stairwell, pulling out my cell and dialling Razors number. I need to get Jamie out of there.

Jamie

It must be psycho bitch day. I watch bullets fly. There's no doubt that Lindsey or Sofia-*fucking bitch needs to pick a name and stick to it,* is the better shot.

Harriet is wounded and bleeding all over Isla's carpets, while Whateverhernameis stands over her.

Thank fuck Isla got out, she saw something in Harriet, she knew what button to press to get these two crazies sparring off.

The gurgle and cough from Harriet tells me one of the bullets has hit something vital. Judging by the blood seeping out the back of her it's gone straight through. I can't help feeling a wave of empathy for her.

"She's dying Sofia," I inform her using her real name. She glares at me briefly, then there's a glimmer of anguish in her gaze before she directs her attention back to Harriet who is now losing color, eyes wide and pleading for help.

"You were my friend, I trusted you. My brother never loved you Christina, the only person Nico loves is Nico, I tried to make you see how bad he was years ago after he got you involved in his plans that day, but you are so fucking obsessed with him. I loved you, you were like a sister. I'm sorry Chrissy I'm so sorry." She falls to her knees next to her and discards her gun to the other side of the room gathering her in her arms, sobbing quietly.

Harriet's weakened gaze meets mine and she tries to mouth something. I kneel close to her.

"Nico-killed-your-dad," she manages to get out, her breathing labored.

"It's ok Chrissy, I'll tell him what happened,

you just rest now." Tear filled eyes meet mine brimming with guilt and regret. The only sound in the room is the rattle of death as Harriet takes her final breath. I wish I could say watching someone die gets easier, but it doesn't; it makes you more aware of the fragility of life. Cold dead eyes look at mine and I gently smooth my hand over her lids to close them.

Silent sobs wrack through Sofia's body as she cradles her friends corpse.

At that moment Razor, Leo and Tiny burst through the door followed closely by a determined and rather pissed looking Isla, I can't help the tug of a smile that pulls at my mouth.

Razor takes one look at the scenario and shakes his head, "Fuck Conroy fuck."

Sofia's head whips up, tearstained cheeks darken as her eyes widen slightly as they land on Razor. If I didn't know better I would say she likes what she sees in my mountain of a friend. Razor's doing some staring of his own.

Her eyes turn cold, the vulnerability replaced by contempt. "I see the cavalry has arrived. Hello Richie, boys, come to take me in for questioning, I'm partial to a good nail ripping. Although, water boarding is my favourite."

Razor looks taken aback by the use of his real name and her bluntness, but quickly regains his usual composure. "Good to know Darlin. You've got yourself into a bit of a situation here haven't ya?"

Sofia laughs humorlessly in agreement; more tears escape her eyes as she looks down at her friend. "Sh-she was my friend."

Me and Razor share a look of understanding, you had to be a heartless bastard if offing one of your own didn't bother you. Razor's eyes soften in a way I've never seen before. "Come on Darlin, my men here will take care of your friend, I think it's time for you to talk don't you?" Sofia just nods brokenly, more tears fall as she let's Leo take Harriet from her.

Isla walks past me her face solemn as she disappears into her room, returning moments later with a blanket which she throws over Sofia's shoulders helping her up. "Let's go and get you cleaned up then we can talk." Isla tells her in a soft voice.

"If she tries anything-"

"She's in shock Jamie, Nico has been using her too. I'll be fine," she snaps, putting me in my place as she leads Sofia into her bedroom, leaving the door ajar. I stare at the door for a moment allowing everything that's just happened to sink in.

I have to end things with Isla. I have to let her go. That could have easily have been her lying dead today, she wouldn't be in any danger if it wasn't for my family's history with the Cartel, Nico would have just left her to carry on believing he was Kevin.

"Let Wild Cat do her thing Conroy, we've got shit to discuss." Razor's voice pulls me away from my thoughts, I grimace.

"Yeah, we do. I now know who killed my dad."

Razors brows rise, and he lets out a sigh "Shit."

CHAPTER TWENTY-TWO

Isla

Life sucks, it completely sucks. I bag the bloodstained clothes up as Sofia showers, sobbing as she scrubs at her flesh, leaving nasty red marks on her perfect skin; no amount of soap is going to wash away the pain or the guilt she must be going through.

She hasn't said much, but it seems Nico has played a lot of people for a long time, I feel a little better knowing I wasn't the only fool that was taken in by his lies.

I hold a towel open for her which she steps into. "Sofia, you need to get dressed so we can talk," I remind her softly. She looks at me, fresh tears brim, threatening to spill.

"Marcus is going to kill me when he finds out what Nico has been doing, he warned him not to draw attention to himself again after he had his men cut up those cops. Isla, I don't want to die." Her voice breaks, "I didn't know my brother was trying to overthrow him, I swear I didn't." She searches my face for some kind of answer or redemption to the chaos flying around in that head of hers, but I don't have the answer. I can't erase all the bad shit that's happened, all I can offer her is some comfort.

A small dry laugh leaves her as she sits on my bed pulling the towel tighter to her curves. "My brother fell for you, you know, I can see why, you're kind and you care about people. I thought he was going give up this life and choose you, you made him so happy, he was a better man when he was playing Kevin; for a while I saw the boy he used to be. Something has changed in him this last year though, he's cold and distant now. "

I frown, what was she telling me, that Nicholai Flores had loved someone other than himself? *Yeah right*, pigs and flying come to mind.

"What about Jamie? Where does he come into all of this?"

She looks at her hands again and plays with her fingers. "His dad was your all-American hero when it came to cracking cases for the police. It was Nico's job to contact the drug suppliers and organize the meet up, Mike Conroy got wind of the meet and had the place stormed by the DEA. Nico and Marcus got away, but one of Nico's best friends was killed in the shoot-out, Nico went after Conroy against Marcus's orders and killed him in cold blood, he dumped his body in the river. They went into hiding after that, you know the rest, Christina went undercover at the Conroy building to report back if Jamie started asking questions about his dad's involvement with the Cartel and

Nico became Kevin and met you. He wanted me to befriend you, Joanna is the name I use for modelling, because well my family name isn't exactly good for a resume and it was my dream from when I was young, so that wasn't completely false. As for Jamie, that started a few months before Harriet interfered. I was just supposed to help distract Jamie, he had started to get restless and Christina said he had started becoming more focused in finding his dad's killer, I don't know what she was thinking involving you. Jamie was good with our casual hook-up, but you know Jamie he is a closed book about relationships he never wanted more with me, he seems to be really into you though." Another dry laugh leaves her. "Truth is I enjoyed being Lindsey, he's not a bad guy and he's not bad in the sack either." I nod, pushing aside the jealousy that gnaws at me at the thought of them together; she wasn't wrong about Jamie, he was a hard nut to crack.

"What if you go to Marcus and tell him what your brother has been doing?" I ask her.

I open the walk-in wardrobe and grab jeans and a shirt for her, I place them next to her on the bed.

She chews on her lip, her face shifts apprehensively as she contemplates what I am suggesting.

"That would mean I am condemning my brother," she says hesitantly.

"Your brother condemned himself a long

time ago Sofia." I say passing her some underwear; my tone is more harsh than I intend, but I get my point across. "I can go with you, that way he'll know you're not lying," I declare.

She looks a little shocked at my suggestion, she considers my idea. She's like a lamb thrown into a world of wolves, scared and alone; I don't think she is built for that life, she's learnt to act tough but the facade is slipping, she looks worn out, a far cry from the fresh faced beauty I called my friend not so long ago.

"Was that the first time you've killed someone?" I ask, she shakes her head.

"It was my third, but the first one that mattered." She looks at her hands again, it's like she can see the blood flowing over her fingers. "The others were during a crossfire when I was younger, we were ambushed by two rival gang members–I thought I had finished killing after them, I'm not cut out for this. I told Nico I would help bring you in but then I was done–I'm sorry for everything Isla, even though it was all pretend I grew to like you, I enjoyed being your friend. You're kind and funny, under different circumstances." She shrugs."But you were just a decoy for my stupid brother."

A loud knock makes us both jump and the door is opened. Jamie's eyes search mine full of questions.

"We've got word of where Nico is. I need you to stay here. Three of Razors guys are here and there's more downstairs. I don't know how long I'll be." His tone is back to being business-like, but I can see the battle in his eyes.

"Can I talk to you a moment please?" I ask keeping my voice low.

He nods. "There's something I have to clear up with you too," he says not quite meeting my eye.

"I'll be back in a moment Sofia, get dressed."

I step back into my sitting room, stunned at how clean it is, there's no sign of blood or the woman who's corpse had filled my floor not half an hour ago.

Razors men were efficient at cleaning up bodies. I didn't want to think of what that entailed.

I lead Jamie to my spare bedroom away from the prying eyes of Leo, Tiny and another guy I am not familiar with. They all watch me suspiciously but I am past giving a shit what they think and besides this was still my home. Razor is talking on the phone with someone and gives Jamie a wave as I lead him into the small room.

As soon as the door clicks closed I step into Jamie wrapping my arms around his torso, after what Sofia just told me about his father I feel like I need to comfort him in someway, he's been through so much in his life. His whole body goes rigid as if I've physically assaulted him.

"Please don't," he says, unwrapping my arms from around his waist and stepping back, his eyes hard and cold. "This isn't right. You're my client, I am not cut out for relationships, you knew this when you met me. It's over Isla, I can't do this-us anymore."

And there it is, the heart-wrenching truth that is Jamie Conroy, I knew this day would come but I hadn't expected it this early or done this coldly especially after what we had already experienced together. I won't belittle myself by making a fuss about it though.

"Fine" I say, determined to keep it together, he's hurting and scared, I'd call bullshit on this entire bravado he's got going on right now. For such a tough guy this was a cowards move, the idea of commitment scared the shit out of him. "It was fun while it lasted," I say harshly. Something flashes in his eyes for a split second and I see that vulnerability there before they are back to hard and cold. "Now we've got that out of the way, I thought you should know, me and Sofia are going to see Marcus. It seems Nico's boss is unaware of his intentions–" Jamie opens his mouth to argue, I raise my hand to stop him. "You're fired as my PI Mr Conroy, our business is done, I'll see to it you recieve all that you are owed for your services. I thank you for your help but I think this got a little too personal, that is a mistake I won't be repeating. Now, if you don't mind I have to get ready, there's a Cartel boss I need to meet and I couldn't possibly do it in bloodstained sweats." I smile coldly at him holding my chin up. "You know your way out." I walk to the door and open it indicating he follows, I watch as his jaw ticks.

"Isla, he'll kill you on sight." Jamie says as he reaches me his face so close to mine, my facade nearly slips as regret fills his eyes "Look I-"

"No need to worry about my safety anymore Mr Conroy you are just the hired help. My life and what I do with it is none of your concern, I hope you bring your father's murderer to justice." I am shocking myself with how well my voice is holding out, the pained expression on his face is enough to make me want to wrap my arms around him again, but I know this is for the best, he needs to focus on getting his dad's killer while I need to make sure the Cartel take the man I have fallen in love with off their hit list.

"Isla please-"

"Goodbye Mr Conroy." I step out of the room and close the door behind me.

Time to pull my big girl panties up and get my life back.

CHAPTER TWENTY-THREE

Jamie

"She fucking called me the hired help." I complain to Razor on the way to Nico's location, I am still reeling from Isla's unexpected response, I thought she would at least shed a tear. It was a first for me to not quite read what someone was thinking, but Isla had surprised me a few times now with her reactions, the girl had me pissed as hell.

Razor chuckles deep in his chest. "Girls got some balls on her, you sure you don't want to tail her yourself, make sure she doesn't get into trouble?"

I shake my head, "Just make sure your men report back with regular updates, I have to get to this location before nightfall so I can work out a plan."

I check the clock on the dashboard, it's fourteen hundred hours, we've been on the road for twenty minutes.

"Are your sources certain he's going to be at the San Pedro shipyard tonight?" I ask.

"They've never been wrong before. There's a drug shipment coming in, Nico wants the biggest cut; he set up the meeting with the suppliers last week. I swear Conroy the guy seriously has a death wish; this deal is happening under Marcus's nose."

"Really? Nico has been busy," I answer him thoughtfully. Maybe there's an easier way to do this.

I chew on it for a few minutes, there's so many scenarios in my head each one always ends with Nico laying in a pool of his own blood. I'll have to see layout of the dock but I have a plan. "I have an idea." Razor gives me a raised eyebrow side-eye, he knows what it's like when I make a plan, "If I can get Isla on board we could bring the entire Cartel down tonight, you still got any ex-Military contacts?"

"Shit Conroy I know that look," Razor declares with a smirk as he pulls out his phone looking rather please with himself "Just give me ten minutes."

I take my mobile out and dial Isla's number willing her not to reject the call.

Isla

I smooth my black pencil dress down and adjust the clutch in my hand as I step out of the cab in front of the huge gated villa in one of the more prestigious neighborhoods in Beverly Hills. Sofia climbs out after me wearing one of my tailored suits, she looks phenomenal. She has an air about her; cool and arrogant, a trait I always assumed was due to her being an established model, now I know different. I suppose associating yourself with powerful men had its advantages for her self-esteem. The confident gal Infront of me now was a far-cry from the sobbing mess a few hours ago. There's a determination in her that I've never seen before.

After discovering her brother is a lying scumbag and has betrayed everyone including his own blood, she's on board with the plan to take Nico down.

"You ready to meet Marcus?" I raise my brows at her question and she grins wide. "He's not what you expect, trust me."

My grip tightens on my clutch as I try to calm my erratic heartbeat, trusting these people is what dragged me into this in the first place, I nearly married one of them for fucksake.

The last week has been a test to my resilience, maybe meeting Jamie Conroy has given me a brand new way to deal with my anxiety issues and the boat load of inconveniences that go with it, this doesn't feel as daunting as it usually would. I've obviously been desensitised with all the shit that's happened. It can't get much worse can it? Who would have thought getting shot at and kidnapped would build my resolve?

"I gotcha Girl," Sofia tells me and winks as she presses the intercom with her perfectly manicured pink nail.

The gate opens straight away. I'm suddenly

regretting agreeing to this plan as three burly men with big guns greet us on the driveway wasting no time in thoroughly patting us down.

"At least by me a drink first," I jest to the hulk of a man rubbing his hands down my backside, he doesn't even acknowledge my attempt to lighten the mood; I can't seem to curb my Louisiana twang today, but what the hell I'll just go with it. I'm tired of trying to be something I'm not.

"Ok boys we're obviously not packin, you're just havin a grope now and that's not ok." They let go of us at Sofia's aggressive tone. "Go and tell Marcus we have some news for him, it's something he's going to need to know." Sofia orders, one of the men disappear into the house following her instructions, she looks so at ease here.

"Ain't you Nico's woman?" One of the muscles asks, looking me up and down with a appreciative glint in his eye.

"Not anymore I ain't, my name's Isla pleased to meet ya." I say in my sweetest Southern drawl holding out my hand, he doesn't take it. I drop my arm and shrug keeping up the bravado but my insides are begging me to get out of this situation before I get shot in the face.

"Samo stop being an asshole and say hello to the lady," Sofia snaps. I flash a smile of appreciation her way.

"I don't trust her, someone as pretty as her always has something to hide," *shit.*

"Well someone as ugly as you shouldn't be

so picky, didn't Mama Samo ever teach you manners?" He grunts at her course tone, she's not impressed with being grunted at, her brows furrow and her hand moves to her hip her free hand wagging a finger at Samo,   "Besides, it's not up to you who to trust here is it eh? I trust her and so will Marcus after today, so watch yourself Samo, or you might find yourself face down in a gutter somewhere missing those big balls of yours."

The other heavy starts sniggering. Samo's face grows increasingly redder, he doesn't like being undermined by a girl.

"Stop terrorising my men Sofia!"

We all look towards the booming voice of Marcus Ravenstone. My breath catches in my throat as I lay my eyes on the most dangerously gorgeous man I've ever seen.

Sofia is pulled into a warm hug, which I suspect affects her a lot more than it does him judging by the flush warming her cheeks.

"I was just telling Samo here to be a bit more polite to your guest Marcus," Sofia complains. Her voice is a little huskier than before, not that I blame her *sheesh*, the guy was distracting.

His eyes finally land on me and something flashes across them before he walks towards me taking my hand. I can't stop my own cheeks from heating at his stare. "And who's this enchanting beauty?" He has warm eyes and a friendly smile, was this man really capable of selling human beings and hacking up cops?

"Please to meet you, I'm Isla, Isla Sussex."

"The pleasure is all mine Miss Isla Sussex. Now I hear you have some information for me?" He purrs never taking his ocean colored eyes off mine; he's intense.

"I do" I say, it's almost a whisper.

"Well then please follow me. I am intrigued to know what Nicholai has been up to while I've been away; I can see now why he was eager to get back to you, you really are a beauty."

I flush again, he was definitely a charmer. I had to remind myself what this man could do and with the information I am about to drop I am certain this gentleman act wouldn't last long. I swallow hard.

"I can assure you Marcus, Nico never came back to me, he's a liar and a deceitful pig and it looks like he's played you too."

His face changes. He glares over at Sofia, murder in his gaze.

"What has your fucking brother done now Sofia? Start talking before I blow a hole in that pretty head of yours."

CHAPTER TWENTY-FOUR

Isla

"Nico is planning on double crossing you Marcus, he wants to over throw you. There's a big deal going down tonight at the San Pedro Shipyard, he's meeting with one of the big suppliers, him and Christina Roberts have been playing you for years, I only found out recently through Isla here." Sofia explains to a furious looking Marcus. The man is terrifying, how Sofia is holding her nerve is beyond me.

"What does she mean, what involvement do you have in all of this?" He snarls at me. I swallow the lump in my throat and look to Sofia, she looks just as scared her eyes beg me to answer him. "Well?"

"Harriet–I mean Christina sent me an anonymous letter with a picture of Nico sitting in a car next to you. It said on the letter that Kevin was still alive, and I had to go to The Rocco club in Lincoln Heights and ask for Conroy, so I did. I only found out when I met him that he was a private investigator. Y-you have to understand my fiancé had disappeared without a trace for months, I was desperate, so to find someone who could give me answers...it was such a relief after months of feeling helpless. It turns out Christina was stirring trouble, she was jealous because Nico still had feeling for me. She got me involved with Conroy to ensure he would feel betrayed and want me dead too, then she could have him to herself; it back fired on her, Nico tried to have Mr Conroy killed and kidnapped me, h-he was going to sell me f-for sex, but I got away. Christina admitted Nico was the one who killed Mike Conroy four years ago. Sofia k-killed her earlier today in my apartment." I open my bag and pull out the photocopies of the letter and image and hold it out to Marcus with shaking hands, he snatches the paper off me and studies it.

"How long has your brother been planning on overturning me Sofia?" He asks without lifting his head from the letter.

Two of his men grab Sofia roughly holding her arms as Marcus slams the letter down on his coffee table and begins pacing slowly in front of her, his movements are predatory, then without warning he slaps her hard, her head whips to the side, a red bruise already starting on her cheek.

"I swear Marcus I don't know, I-I thought he was loyal to you, that's why I am here, you needed to know before he does something to harm you. Marcus please, you know I would never do anything to hurt you, I love you." He grabs her under her chin and brings his face close to hers, curses then he kisses her aggressively, before stepping away and pacing across the room to the window.

"Let her go, she's telling the truth." She is released immediately, she slumps to the floor, tears leave black streaks down her cheeks as she sobs openly. I want to run to her to offer comfort, but I know these men won't allow it.

"Giorgio, Carlos get my men together, one of our brothers and his men need putting down." He looks over at me, "is your Mr Conroy after revenge for his father?"

I nod, "I think so, he's at the shipyard now, he's planning on taking Nico out, The Maw of Fenris MC are helping him, the Vice President served in the Marines with Mr Conroy."

Marcus looks impressed. "Ah, Razor, we've had a few dealings with their president Harker. They are always good for extra security if we need it. Razor on the other hand we've never had much to do with him, obviously he's educated in our affairs though if he's been helping Conroy." He turns back to the window lost in thought. "Do you know how long I've known Nicholai Flores Miss Sussex?" I shake my head. "Thirty-two years. We grew up together. In all that time he's been my brother, our parents were friends, we used to play together as children. Not once in all that time would I have believe he would ever carve holes into my back. That image you have of us, it was the first time I had seen him in three years, we only spoke on the phone before then. I've been away taking care of family affairs. We laughed together and caught up, he told me about the woman who had stolen his heart, said he was going to marry her and go straight. You're telling me he never came back to you?" I shake my head, tears fill my eyes, even now the deceit cracks something inside of me.

"I received that picture two weeks after it was taken, he had been missing for four months. I thought he was dead. The cops couldn't find any trace of him. Before then, he was always away on business with work, as you know he was a exceptional accountant." He watches me but makes no move to interrupt or deny, he wants me to continue. "I have found out recently Nico and his men have been trafficking women and selling them to the highest bidder as well as dealing cocaine . This supplier he is meeting with today is big league-"

There's a knock on the door, two men enter, they are just as big as the other two that left before.

"The cars are ready Mr Ravenstone," they announce, Marcus nods at them.

"Thank you, Miss Sussex your honesty is refreshing, this issue will require my immediate attention. Sofia, Miss Sussex, you are both coming with me." Marcus declares before indicating to his men to escort us out.

Jamie

The dockyard is eerily quiet when we finally get there, the shipment isn't due for an hour, so we have enough time to organize ourselves. I study the layout of the perimeter and the best places I need to position the guys to have a good shot. Razor as usual has out done himself with the backup I requested. Six ex-marines have shown up, two of them from our platoon in Afghanistan. A truck full of rifles has just arrived and Razor is barking orders to his own men while handing out the impressive selection of weaponry.

The next thirty minutes fly by, everyone is in position out of sight and awaiting my signal, the sound of the approaching cargo ship is the only noise that can be heard. Razor sits next to me behind some cargo crates we've filled full of more ammunition. A vibrating from Razors pocket makes us both jump. Razor pulls it out and reads the message, before tucking his phone back in his pocket. There's an in-take of breath and a look of utter devastation on my friends face before his eyes harden and his jaw sets again.

"Anything to worry about Bud?" I ask.

"Nothing that can't wait until this is done." There's something in the huskiness of his voice that tells me whatever that message was about has upset him more than he's letting on, it must be something serious. Razor never lets anything affect him, he was normally resilient to shit that would make most men cry like babies so seeing even the slightest concern on his face meant something terrible had gone down.

His jaw ticks and there's a look on his face I haven't seen since Afghanistan after that bus explosion.

The sound of approaching cars pulls both of our attention back to the dockyard and our mission, our focus now back in the game. Two Mercedes with blacked out windows pull into the dockyard, the engines are cut but the headlights throw beams of light on to the side of the ship, no one makes a move to get out of the cars.

There's movement from on board the vessel and a metal gangway is released. Three men ascend down the gangway steps they are all dressed in expensive looking suits. There are snipers on board the ship, all trained on the cars, these fuckers weren't taking any chances with the Cartel either.

The door to the Mercedes opens and out steps Nico and his four-armed back-up. There are a few words spoken and a handshake before him and his men are led on board.

"The feds will be here soon, there's still no sign of Marcus, I thought for sure he'd want to see this deal for himself," I wonder.

As if on cue the dockyard is suddenly filled with more cars, too many to count, they are all black and everyone has blacked out windows. One of the car doors opens and out steps a broad dark-haired guy wearing a black suit, he a mean looking bastard.

"Shit JC, that's Marcus, Wild Cat came through for us," Razor whispers.

Marcus turns and holds out his hand, a blond head appears, and I nearly drop my rifle, he brought her with him.

"Razor, he's got Isla, fuck, he's going to use her to get to Nico, I have to get onto that boat."

CHAPTER TWENTY-FIVE

Isla

The air is thick with anticipated danger, trouble is brewing in the worst possible way and I am stuck in the center of it.

Six-gun shots sound out behind us as me and Sofia are led towards the floating vessel illuminated by the many headlights of the Cartel's vehicles.

Marcus ordered Nico's men to be killed as soon as we got here, he didn't listen to reasoning when they begged for their lives, as far as he was concerned, they were part of the scheme to deceive him. Now, there's little to no emotion in Marcus's face, he doesn't even flinch as more rounds are fired, killing off any one still moving. I jump with every loud bang as they penetrate the night air, I don't think I'll ever get used to that sound.

Marcus grips my arm, not enough to hurt but enough for me to know there is no escaping my fate. Part of me wants to see Nico again to get closure, but I know he isn't going to give me the gratification of being even remotely sorry for what he has put me through. He's sick, twisted and rotten to the core, the only place for him now is prison or death if Marcus and Jamie get their way. I can't help but feel a little disappointed at that notion, Jamie deserves to find some justice for his father's untimely death, he should be the one to land a bullet between Nico's eyes.

It's looking likely that Marcus is going to get to him first though.

The metal steps clink underneath my stiletto heels and for a second I feel as if I will lose my balance, I grip on to the railing with my free hand. Sofia seems as confident as usual and keeps looking behind giving me reassuring glances, her offer of support does nothing for the anxiety building in my stomach, I feel sick with nerves.

We finally reach the deck of the ship.
We are met with an angry looking Nico and a man I can only assume is the supplier he was here to meet. Four men with big guns stand behind him looking ready to open fire with just a nod. The smug grin that suddenly appears on Nico's face tells me everything-this was a set up.
"You came, I knew you would Marcus. Have you met our new supplier?" Nico asks, there's a madness in his eyes, "you do know though don't you, he's not really a supplier? This was all a rouse to get you here, and you brought my fiancé with

you too, this day is getting better and better; I told you she was beautiful didn't I?" His eyes land on me. "Hello Buttercup, you wore black, you must have guessed we were having a funeral today."

"Yes, yours, you sick bastard," I snarl. He throws his head back and laughs like I've just told him the funniest joke ever.

The click of a safety clip being removed stops his hearty chuckle and his eyes are on one of Marcus's men behind us, the sound of dozens of guns being trained on us has Marcus releasing my arm from his death grip.

"Now, now Marcus, tell Giorgio to put his gun away before one of my many snipers take his head." Nico suggests smirking widely. Marcus turns and nods at Giorgio who lowers his gun. "Good to see you know who's in control here." Nico's sights are back on me. "I have missed you Buttercup." His eyes turn to Sofia, "Sister, you did well, I am impressed. I knew you'd go running to Marcus, you never were loyal."

"Fuck you Nicholai," Sofia spits. "Christina is dead by the way, I blew a hole in her stomach."

The harshness of her tone and the stubbornness in her both impress and terrify me, I can tell by Nico's face it has rattled him too. His scowl quickly turns into another sinister grin directed at Sofia. "So she told you our little plan then?" He sneers.

"Yeah, she told me how you murdered Mike Conroy and had all those cops chopped up you sick fuck... She set Isla up with Conroy investigations because she knew it would get a reaction out of you, at least you didn't disappoint her; you should have stuck with her, you two deserved each other, both fucking deluded." Sofia is raging now, her fists are clenched, and she's twitchy. I really hope she doesn't pounce because he'll have her shot.

"I've been calling the shots for a while Sofia, you always were naive. Kevin was my alias so I could build up my contacts and as for Conroy he's just an inconvenience, he'll meet the same fate as his interfering father-"

Suddenly, a shot rings out from the dock and one of Nico's men falls from his position above us narrowly missing Marcus, who moves out of the way quickly.

"Take them out, take them all out!" Nico yells and makes a grab for me, I try to run but I am not quick enough, he catches my hair and yanks me into him dragging me behind some crates and through a door.

I claw at his arm and try to throw punches, the grip on my hair burns my scalp.

He pulls a gun out and presses it against my temple, my entire world freezes and I stop struggling, I don't want to die.

"Play nice or I'll blow your fucking brains out."

Jamie

I'm at the front end of the ship at last, staying hidden amongst crates has been the easy part, now I had to get on this fucking boat without being seen, one mistake and I would be full of bullet holes.

I scour the area looking for anything I can use to climb up on without being spotted; there's nothing. I am going to have to take my chances on the gangway and hope Razors guys cover my ass.

The sound of gunfire on board grows more aggressive, these fuckers weren't playing. It sounds like an active warzone up there. I take the steps quickly my Glock ready to take anyone out who gets in my way.

I reach the top and peer round, there are bodies scattered all over the deck from both sides; it's a bloodbath. I spot Marcus hiding close to the gangway behind a crate another man next to him sitting holding a bloody bullet wound in his shoulder. Marcus is taking shots at one of the snipers on the bridge. I've got a clear shot. I aim and fire. I get him in face and he drops to the deck with the other corpses. Marcus whips his head around, aiming his weapon. I see the same stubbornness reflected back at me, this fucker would die fighting for his life, I keep my gun trained on him, neither of us blink.

"Where's Isla?" I ask. His features change,

and he lowers his gun.

"Conroy?" The look of relief is evident on his face for a split second before his features harden again.

"Yeah. Where is she?" I reply lowering my weapon as I approach him.

"Nicholai dragged her off through a door behind some crates over there." He points towards two crates about eight yards away.

"There's too many of them, I won't make it, can you cover me?"

"Yeah, go now. I'll hold them off best I can."

I nod my thanks and get ready to make my move, Marcus looks over the crate and shoots, more gunfire travels in his direction. I make a run for it, dodging bullets as I go. A burning sensation rips through my left bicep as a bullet grazes my flesh, I keep moving, I reach the door and pull it open.

Sofia stands on the other side noticeably shaken up, her face and clothes are covered in blood. "Jamie, you came?" She looks relieved, like I'm her salvation.

"Are you hurt?" I ask, not really that concerned for her wellbeing, bitch deserves everything she gets.

"Apart from a few cuts and bruises I'm fine." I nod at her answer looking her up and down.

"Where did Nico take Isla?" I ask, she looks disappointed, did she really think I would come for her? Has she got a short memory.

"He dragged her down there," she points down the corridor. "Is she really worth risking your life for though Jamie? Nico will shoot you on sight."

I glare at her, "He's got the woman I love doing God-knows-what to her, I'll fucking die saving her if I have too, your brother doesn't get to have her." I shake my head at her lack of empathy. "I wouldn't expect a deceitful bitch like you to understand." She looks hurt and I don't give a shit. I am bored with this conversation, "Wait here, Razor and his men will be here soon, they'll get you out if you're still breathing."

Her expression changes, the idea of my friend turning up pleases her. "Oh good, a real man coming to my rescue. Go and get your Isla back, and try not to get that pretty head of yours blown off."

"Darlin this is a routine day out in the field for this PI. Good luck getting out." I say as I wink and head down the corridor my gun raised.

CHAPTER TWENTY-SIX

Isla

My feet ache from being dragged in these stupid heels, Nico is scared shitless, reckless and unpredictable. He currently has me pressed against a crate on the front end of the ship trying to sweet talk me into believing he can give me the world.

"You'll love the life I can give you Buttercup, the life we had before that was pretend, but not the way I feel about you, I never faked that Buttercup, now you know who I am you'll have the best of everything, no one else will ever look after you as good as I can, no one will touch you, I'll take their hands if they dare."

I am feeling reckless myself right now, I'm tired of being scared.

"Like Jamie Conroy has you mean?" I blurt out. His eyes darken. I knew hearing that name would get a reaction, he glares at me.

"What has that Fucker got to do with us?" He growls.

I smirk at him, I am sure I look certifiable.

"He's got everything to do with me because he's the man I want not you, you're pathetic and half the man he is. He touched me you know and I loved every single second of his hands on my body; I would pay to watch you even try and take just one of his fingers-"

A sharp slap across my face, leaves a metallic taste in my mouth. I hold my cheek shocked for a second and then I laugh hysterically, not quite sure what I am doing or what is actually happening. I guess when you finally don't care if you live or die nothing can faze you, I think I just finally reached that point, obviously this must be the way I'm handling it.

Nico looks at me like I've gone insane; he's not wrong. I spit the blood out of my mouth into his face, determined to get him to hit me again, he doesn't even flinch or move to clean it off his cheek. I look at him wiping my mouth smirking. "He fucked me good and hard, gave me my first orgasm ever, he's so much better than you in bed, he even has a bigger dick than you 'Kevin'. You really think I would want you now after having him."

He looks like I have crushed his heart into pieces, his eyes search mine like he's looking for a sign that I am kidding; all he sees is dead eyes that are a reflection of my dead heart. Nothing matters anymore, he can kill me, I'm ready for this all to end one way or another.

His eyes are suddenly full of fury as Reality

registers.

"You whore, you fucking whore, you are mine, I will slaughter anyone who comes within a meter of you." he shakes me hard and presses the gun to my temple.

"Do it, blow my fucking brains out, I'm never going to be yours." I push my head against the barrel of his gun and stare at him defiantly.

He hesitates for a second like he's trying to decide what to do with me. Suddenly, the gun is pulled away and he slams the handle of the gun into my head hard. Pain like I've never felt before erupts in my skull, I feel like the trauma from the blow has ripped a hole in my head, everything spins, he does it again harder this time and my world turns dark.

Jamie

Razor is finally on board, I can hear his booming vocals ordering his men to open fire, he will tear through Nico's men like skittles. The Maw of Fenris didn't take prisoners either, so anyone they find will die. Marcus will owe the MC big time after this.

Now, I just need to get my girl and we can go home; it's easier said than done with this slippery bastard though. I don't know how but he's managed to always stay one step ahead all this time, well not today, today Isla gets her life back and I get justice for my Dad.

Nicholai Flores is a dead man walking.

I head for the front end of the ship through the bridge, there's another door, I open it cautiously, there's stairs leading to the accommodation and control room.With my Glock raised I hurry to the other side of the room. I pull open the door and scan the area my gun ready.

Satisfied there's no one here I step into the warm night, the sky is alive with the flash of gunfire. I creep slowly around the crates my senses alert, stealth is everything in this situation. There's rustling and a muffled voice coming from the other side of this crate.

"Wake up, come on I didn't hit you that hard. I've got a boat waiting for us. Come on, that's it open your eyes, don't look at me like that. You made me hit you Isla, you pushed at the wrong buttons Buttercup."

"Kevin? Urgh, Nico my head hurts." Her beautiful voice is groggy and strained.

The fucker hit her, she sounds weak and terrified. I feel rage bubble inside me. I fight every natural instinct to end the motherfucker. I breathe through my nose to steady the need to rush this, I need to bide my time, catch him off guard.

"Nico, you made it." There's someone else here? That voice sounds really familiar, was that one of Razors MC guys? "The boat's ready, you need some help with the female?"

"Did you plant those explosives?" Explosives? *Fuck*. I'll have to warn Razor, I pull my phone out and shoot him a quick text praying he gets it.

"Yeah, they are due to go off in fifteen minutes like we planned, I told you I would sort it. Offing Harker was easy, the fucker didn't even know it was coming. Razor thinks he was killed working a job."

"You did well Chip, Razor never suspected a thing."

A gun is fired and Isla whimpers like the sound causes her pain. He just shot Chip. Razor was going to be pissed he didn't get to end the snake himself. That must have been what that message was he got earlier *Fuck*.

"Get the fuck up now Isla, this boat is going up soon I intend to be out of here before that happens."

I've heard enough.

I run round the side of the crate gun pointed. Something hard hits me on the back of my head. *Shit*. I didn't see that coming. I turn and punch my assailant in the face, he moves and grips me round my waist wrestling me to the floor he pummels me in the face. I manage to unclip the blade strapped to my thigh and ram it into his side, pull it out and ram it into his chest, yank it out and ram it into his neck. Shock registers with my first blow now his eyes are glazed as he falls off me, unmoving.

I stand, facing Nico, his gun pressed to the side of Isla's face, as he backs towards the railings were a rope ladder hangs.

I take a step towards him, and his grip on Isla intensifies

"I'll fucking kill her then neither of us can have her," he sneers. "Climb down to the boat or I'll put a bullet in Mr Conroy here," he snarls into Isla's bloodstained hairline. I clench my fists, every fiber of me wants to beat this fucker to death. Isla nods, scared eyes watch me wide and glistening with unshed tears.

"Good girl," he tells her releasing her. She climbs over the railings her eyes never leave mine, once she's out of sight I turn on Nico, who now has his gun trained on me.

"I'm impressed, you are much tougher than your old man, he didn't give me half the trouble you have," he chuckles to himself. "Fuckin Christina and her jealousy. I would have come back for Isla, I was planning on coming back when Christina decided to get you involved, I knew it wouldn't be long until she was in your bed, I know how you work with women. Isla's different though isn't she? She gets under your skin, makes you want more. You've tasted her, you know how fuckin sweet she is, and that innocence in her, *damn*, it made me want to go straight for a while, but guys like us we don't get happy ever afters do we Conroy?"

What did this sicko want a fucking heart to heart?

I laugh humorlessly, "I wouldn't have left her in the first place Dickhead, not if she was mine. You don't deserve her, neither of us do; she deserves to be with someone who treats her like the angel she is, she shouldn't be treated like property." I lower my gun. "Come on Nico, put the gun down, let's see how fucking tough you really are, instead of hiding behind that piece of metal." I goad him.

"You love her don't you?" His voice is hard and full of malice. He's going to fire I can read him like a book, the flick of his eyes to the trigger, the slight stiffening of his composure as he gets himself ready to take the shot, this asshole was too predictable.

"Someone like you could never comprehend what I feel for Isla." I tell him.

His eyes change and the gun goes off.

I dive out of the way, moving quickly towards him, knocking the gun out of his hand before he can react, I slam my fist into his jaw feeling the bone crack as his head whips to the side.

My next blow is blocked, and I swipe his leg, but he stands strong, he throws a punch of his own and connects, I manage to dodge his fist enough, so it causes minimal damage to my cheekbone. I throw my body weight on him and wrestle him to the ground we go blow for blow every fist counting.

I manage to work him into a choke hold and I nearly have him unconscious, he pulls a concealed blade out from his shirt and sticks me right in my thigh, I bellow in agony as the metal slices through my muscle. I don't let go of him, but my grip loosens slightly. I've got the fucker exactly where I want him now.

I wince as I pull the blade out a guttural roar of grief, anger and retribution leaves me as I move my arm and slit his throat viciously. Shock and then defeat crosses his eyes at my quick reflexes, the light dims in his wide gaze and he gurgles his last breath. I wish I could bask in this moment, but I don't have time, the explosives will be going off any minute.

I drag myself away from him and stand putting all the weight on my good leg.

Suddenly, a massive explosion rips through the ship tearing up everything it touches. I sprint to the railings and throw myself overboard before the fire ball engulfs the entire vessel.

I feel heat hit my back as I throw myself into the deep dark waters of the Pacific Ocean.

CHAPTER TWENTY-SEVEN

Isla

I watch in horror as Nico pulls a blade from inside his suit jacket plunging it into Jamie's leg, Jamie had the upper hand before. Jamie pulls the knife out of his leg blood pools around the wound, he slits Nico's throat, I watch as the man I loved for four years take his last breath. I thought I would feel sadness or something to account for all the tears I cried when he disappeared, but the only feeling I get is one of relief as watch him die.

I know I mustn't have long before the explosives go off, but I needed to make sure Jamie got out alive, the thought of a world without him in it causes dread to fester in my stomach.

I move quickly my heels not making this easy. Suddenly, without warning a massive explosion rips through the boat. I am thrown backwards unable to hold on as my world is rocked. I fall and land with an almighty splash, the harsh water stings my skin, the cold takes my breath away. I panic, disorientated. My arms flail in my attempt to stay afloat, salt water fills my lungs making me splutter and choke, it's impossible to do anything but let the currents bend me to their will.

Pieces of debris land in the water around me causing a shift in the directions I am pulled, I am dragged along with the strong waves caused by the vengeful sea. Something hard hits my already battered head from above and my head spins again. I try to cry out in agony but more water fills my lungs.I am going under, too exhausted to fight… I'll let the water have me. I'm tired of fighting. I'll let this all end, there's no way I can withstand the battering my body is getting anyway. It's useless. My head pounds and makes me dizzy.

I'll sink and let the darkness take me, the darkness always wins.

Jamie

I resurface, and suck in a few deep breaths. *Fuck* this water is cold. I frantically kick my legs to stay afloat, the area is lit up with the light from the flames.

I swim towards the small sailboat floating aimless in the midst of the chaos. Isla should be on there. Using all my strength I reach the boat and lift myself to look, it's empty.

Fuck, where is she?

I pull myself up on to the small vessel my eyes scan the turbulent tides caused by falling crates, I spot her, fighting against the rough waves. She hadn't made it to the boat before the explosion hit. *Shit*. Had she even got down that ladder?

"Isla!" I bellow, she doesn't hear me, trapped in a state of panic. The look in her face is one of defeat.

Then suddenly she's gone, swallowed up by the water. My heart drops to my stomach.

"Isla, no!" I dive back into the water ignoring the pain that shoots through my thigh, I swim like leviathan himself is chasing me.

I reach the place she went under within seconds; I gulp in some air filling my lungs and dive under.

I kick and kick, relieved when I finally feel the skin of her arm against my hand, I managed to grab her, I drag her back to the surface and use all my strength to get us back to the little boat, hauling us both in, panting and freezing.

I lie her flat, I am shivering violently but I don't care, Isla isn't breathing. I check for a pulse, there's one but it's weak. I start breathing for her, over and over, if there is God I hope he is a merciful one and brings her back to me.

"Come on baby breathe, please Isla, don't you leave me." I blow a few more puffs of air into her lungs and she splutters to life, I cradle her in my arms, saying a silent thank you to the heavens.

Her beautiful green eyes open and she looks at me, there's a weak smile on her perfect lips.

"Jamie, you're alive," she croaks.

"I am beautiful girl, I'm a hard man to kill." I say kissing her forehead.

She sighs contented and closes her eyes again mumbling "I love you," she falls back into unconsciousness, her breathing becoming labored.

"Fuck! Isla don't you dare. Stay with me. I fucking love you too do you hear me, don't leave. Don't go." My heart shatters as I feel her pulse growing weaker, her body giving up.

Tears fill my eyes and I bellow her name.

Then there's a commotion as lights from a rescue boat blind me. Two men in uniforms climb aboard and Isla's lifeless body is taken from me and carried off.

I sit in the same position for what feels like forever. I can't breathe. I couldn't save her. She's dead and I failed her. I shout words, they are incoherent. Razor is here telling me everything is ok, that I need to go to hospital. I need to let them help me. I don't want their help I want to kill every fucker who touches me, nothing is ok, nothing will ever be ok again. Isla is gone. I watched her die, and I want to be dead too.

I fight as arms pin me down taking swings that miss every time, I bellow her name again in anguish, there's a pin prick in my neck and everything spins before my veins absorb the drug and the darkness encloses.

"Isla, I'm sorry, I'm so fucking sorry I couldn't save you."

CHAPTER TWENTY-EIGHT

Jamie

Isla is in a medical induced coma, there's swelling in her brain, they are not sure if she bumped her head in the fall off the ship or if it was when Nico hit her. The poppy shaped bruise at her temple is a tell-tale sign that she's been hit hard with something blunt, Nico must have hit her with the handle of his gun with some force to cause this much trauma.

I swear I want to bring that bastard back to life so I can beat him to death all over again. I pace back and forth. She has to wake up. I need to tell her how I feel.

Five days they had to keep her under until the swelling started going down. They took her off the sedatives yesterday, but she is still unconscious.

"She'll wake when she's ready, she sustained a huge trauma to her head. You have to be prepared for the worst Mr Conroy, she might not remember a lot that happened." He gives me a sympathetic smile. It might be easier if she has forgotten, the shit she's seen lately would have destroyed a weaker person, not my Isla though she is a warrior, one of life's survivors.

He's the same doctor who treated me when I came in. I had to be taken into surgery to work on my thigh to mend the tissue damage. Apparently, I was less than co-operative. I had to be sedated for them to work on me; it was finding out that I was wrong that pulled me out of that downward spiral into madness. To be told Isla was still alive and fighting, that they had got her heart beating again. I have never been happier to be proven wrong in my entire life. I knew after hearing those amazing words, I had to get strong so I could get back to her.

I want to be the first thing she sees when she opens those gorgeous eyes so I can tell her she's the reason I want to keep on breathing.

"You're both lucky to be alive." I look blankly at the doctor, there was that word again "Lucky." I'll feel lucky once my girl wakes up and I can get us both out of here, did I mention that I fucking hate hospitals.

"You need to rest JC bud." Razor says from the sofa on the other side of the room. How long has he been sitting there? I smile weakly at him, I have two amazing friends. My head goes back to Greg earlier and his excitement about finding a new secretary, he was setting up some interviews. As long as she was'nt a backstabbing whore with a vendetta against me or my family I didn't give a fuck. I wish I could give a shit about that place, I am sure I'll get my buzz back after all this blows over, but until then I know it's in good hand with Greg taking the wheel for a while–I need a fucking vacation.

"Did you hear me, or are you just choosing to be an ignorant asshole." Razor jests breaking through my thoughts. I'm beat but I'll never give in not while my girl's still sleeping.

"I'll sleep once I know she's awake, until then fuck off."

Razor chuckles. "Ok tough guy, but at least go and eat something and take a shower, you smell like shit."

He wasn't lying, I stunk. Maybe getting freshened up wasn't a bad idea and my stomach was protesting something crazy.

"I'll stay with her until you come back," he tells me.

I stand and place a kiss on top of Isla's head "I'll be back soon beautiful girl."

I nod my thanks to Razor feeling a little choked up, he understands and nods back, this has been hell for all of us, he takes my place on the seat next to my girl.

Isla

Six hours later...

Ouch, my head hurts, my mouth is dry and

there's something heavy laying on my hand. I open my eyes, they strain and burn in the light, I squint allowing them to adjust. I'm in a hospital bed, Jamie is sitting bent forward fast asleep with his head resting on top of his hand, his other hand grips mine tightly, little snores leave him and my heart swells, he's been here waiting for me to wake.

How long have I been here? What happened? What was the last thing I remember?

I wrack my brain, but the pounding makes thinking impossible. I groan, protesting loudly. I need some pain relief.

Jamie stirs and lifts his head, tired red rimmed dark eyes meet mine, they brighten when he realises, I'm awake and he's up out of the chair startling me.

"Isla, you're awake? Oh, baby you don't know how long I've prayed to see those beautiful green eyes open." *Baby?*

He stands and presses a button on the wall above my head.

Suddenly, the room is filled with medical staff.

For the next hour I am poked and prodded, and asked so many questions it makes my head spin, I am exhausted and grouchy by the time they're gone but the pain in my head is easier.

ΔΔΔ

My Mum and Clare are here and have been for the last few hours. It's been nearly a week since I was brought in here. The aching in my head isn't as severe as it was, the meds they gave me are working a treat.

Jamie had to go to the office to meet some new staff Greg has hired. I half think he was trying to give me chance to spend time with my family, who are currently both squeezing me so tight and ugly crying.

Apparently, I died twice, they had to resuscitate me; it looks like fate has other plans for me after all.

"I can't believe Kevin was a member of the Cartel." Clare says worrying her bottom lip. "You don't think they'll come back to finish the job do you?" I look at her thoughtfully shaking my head.

"Kevin's real name was Nicholai Flores." Her eyes widen as she recognizes the name. "He was double crossing them; they are going to be glad he's dead." Clare doesn't look pacified by my answer.

"The head of the Cartel owes me one, Wild Cat here helped so they owe her too." Razors voice booms from the doorway making everyone jump, and he winks at a now terrified looking Clare.

"Clare, Mum, meet Razor, Razor, my sister Clare and my Mother Mary Sussex."

"Please to meet you both Mam, you can call me Richie," he says taking my mums hand and kissing the back of it. Did this guy have any limits to his sleaziness. I almost laugh out loud at my Mother's face. "Now I see where Wild Cat here gets her beauty," he purrs and my mother blushes crimson.

"Are you flirting again Razor?" Jamie jokes as he enters the room looking hot and all business-like in his suit. His deep voice sends butterflies into my stomach. A few things have started returning about before I fell unconscious, I am certain I heard him tell me he loved me, but I could have just dreamt it, things are still a little cloudy.

He limps in and warmly greets my mother and sister who are looking a little shell shocked, they soon warm to them though. Jamie is very charming, and Razor is just a big flirt. My mother laps up the attention from the big lummox.

After fussing over me and a good few more tears they leave. Razor follows them out stating he's got stuff to sort out. There's a sadness in him a side I've not seen before now, he's good at hiding his feelings behind humor.

"Is Razor ok?" I ask Jamie who is now back in the chair next to me.

"Razors brother Harker was murdered by Chip one of his MC, Chip was working for Nico. He shot him in the back while they were out on a routine check of their warehouses and he planted those explosives on the ship. Razor has to take his brothers place as President in the MC now; it's not something Razor ever talked about doing, I think he was happy with his brother being in charge; he'll work it out, Razor is adaptable."

He leans forward and takes my hand in his.

"I remember Nico shooting someone called Chip when I came around after he hit me, was that him?"Jamie kisses the back of my hand and nods.

"Oh, poor Razor he must be devastated. What happened to Sofia?" My voice is husky as he plays with my fingers, his touch is distracting my train of thought.

"She got out, Marcus took her with him. Do you really care about her Isla, she was in on it too."

I shake my head at his inability to let things go. "She helped us, I never would have had the balls to face Marcus alone. I think there's some good in her, Nico deceived so many people her included." I remind him.

"I suppose." His lips are back on my hand his mouth gently rubs back and forth. "You see the good in everyone beautiful girl, it's one of the many things I admire about you."

I smile seductively at him letting him know how his touch affects me.

"I thought this thing between us was a mistake Mr Conroy?" His eyebrows raise, there's a playfulness in the depths of his eyes.

"Well you see, I found a brand new case I

wanted to work, it's one that I've never tried before and I thought maybe you might want to help me out with it Miss Sussex?"

I pretend to way up my options.

"What would this new case entail Mr Conroy? Would it be dangerous?" I ask playing along.

"Oh, definitely," he purrs seductively. My insides buzz with anticipation. "It would mean you might have to move out of your apartment."

"Move? Mr Conroy where on Earth would I possibly move to?"

He looks uncertain for a second. "Well there's this PI who kind of needs you to keep him warm of a night, you would both be naked, and it would definitely have to be every day for the rest of your life."

I feel my cheeks warming. "Really? A life time? This sound like a tough case, what will I get in return for spending the rest of my life with this PI?" Tears fill my eyes at what he's suggesting.

I can see the vulnerability in him, this was a first for him, it meant he was finally allowing himself some happiness after everything he had been through. He was starting to believe he deserved to have something more.

He takes a nervous breath. "His love and devotion, I love you beautiful girl," he tells me his voice full of raw emotion.

"I love you too Jamie." A single tear escapes my eye and he swipes it away with the pad of his thumb.

"Sounds like this case is going to be a lot of fun." He grins the playfulness back.

"Yep this one's going to be a life changer Mr Conroy, not your average case."

"Well Miss Sussex, we better get started." Jamie smirks and presses his lips against mine in one of his earth shattering kisses.

"Unless someone like you cares a whole awful lot, nothing is going to get better it's not."
\- Dr Seuss

I hope you enjoyed getting to know Jamie and Isla.

Please let me know what you thought by leaving a review on either Amazon or Goodreads. your feedback is always welcome and helps me to grow as an author.

Liked this story? I also have an ongoing fantasy series available.

@anna-louisedann.com

Please come visit my website for new releases and links to my social media pages, or you can find my books on Amazon and Goodreads.

Thanks for reading.

Much Love Always

Anna-Louise
XXX

Printed in Poland
by Amazon Fulfillment
Poland Sp. z o.o., Wrocław

63231980R00129